RUGBY ROOKIES

Mike Levitt

James Lorimer & Company Ltd., Publishers
Toronto

James Lorimer & Company Ltd., Publishers acknowledges funding support from
the Ontario Arts Council (OAC), an agency of the Government of Ontario.
We acknowledge the support of the Canada Council for the Arts, which
last year invested $153 million to bring the arts to Canadians throughout the
country. This project has been made possible in part by the Government of
Canada and with the support of Ontario Creates.

Cover design: Tyler Cleroux
Cover image: Shutterstock

9781459415744
eBook also available 9781459415737

Cataloguing data for the hardcover edition is available from Library and
Archives Canada.

Library and Archives Canada Cataloguing in Publication (Paperback)

Title: Rugby rookies / Mike Levitt.
Names: Levitt, Mike, 1957- author.
Series: Sports stories.
Description: Series statement: Sports stories
Identifiers: Canadiana (print) 20200356437 | Canadiana (ebook) 20200356445
| ISBN 9781459415720 (softcover) | ISBN 9781459415737 (EPUB)
Classification: LCC PS8623.E949 R833 2021 | DDC jC813/.6—dc23

Published by:	Distributed in Canada by:	Distributed in the US by:
James Lorimer &	Formac Lorimer Books	Lerner Publisher Services
Company Ltd., Publishers	5502 Atlantic Street	241 1st Ave. N.
117 Peter Street, Suite 304	Halifax, NS, Canada	Minneapolis, MN, USA
Toronto, ON, Canada	B3H 1G4	55401
M5V 0M3		www.lernerbooks.com
www.lorimer.ca		

Printed and bound in Canada.
Manufactured by Friesens in Altona, MB in January 2021.
Job #272117

For Kayla, an inspiration to all of us.

Contents

1   Stampeder Pride   7

2   The Pledge   12

3   Big Plans   17

4   Shot Down   24

5   Fail   30

6   One-on-One   36

7   Cop Outs   43

8   Jerks   50

9   Showdown   55

10 Just a Bunch of Girls with a Ball   58

11 Solo   63

12 A Coach with Cred   69

13 Bring It On   77

14	Big Money	82
15	Proof	89
16	All In	94
17	In the League	101
18	Curve Ball	108
19	The Old Rugby Juices	112
20	Game On	116
21	All Heart	121
Acknowledgements		126

1 Stampeder
PRIDE

The biggest guy on the field is like a runaway truck charging down the sideline. The ball crammed under his arm, he launches himself shoulder-first into the closest tackler. The two rain-slick bodies smack together with a slap so loud it shocks me. The defender bounces back, and he splats butt-first into a puddle of mud. The big guy staggers a step. Then he lurches into the next pair of tacklers. They lock arms around his waist and his beefy thighs.

I'm watching safely from the sideline with my three best friends. Half the school comes out when the boys get to play a home game. The bleachers are overflowing and the sidelines are crammed. But this is the first time I've really watched. I think rugby looks like the best game ever. I bet running with the ball is as wild as a hockey breakaway or a fast break in basketball. I'd love it!

Just thinking about playing makes my heart pound. I'm quick. I know that from soccer. And I'm fast. I've got half a dozen hundred-metre sprint medals on my wall.

I could do it! My breath catches in my throat.

The big guy starts falling to the turf but gets a pass away. It's a soft chest pass to the team captain, Ben Horvat. I've known Ben since forever. He's fifteen, a year older than me. Our families get together for Sunday dinners, camping, ski trips. He's like a big brother.

"That's an offload, Maddy," my friend Hailey tells me. "You make a pass just as you're getting hit. Tough to do." Hailey would be a great rugby player. She's super ripped. Hailey sometimes struts like her arms are too buff to fit at her sides.

On the field, Ben looks like he's in trouble. There are defenders coming at him from all sides. He fakes one way, then the other. He finds a sliver of space and takes off, racing downfield.

"Run!" Everleigh is shouting right next to me. "Go, Ben! That's what you wanna do. Go, Stampeders, go!" Everleigh gets excited easily, and she talks a lot. She's one of my best friends. We're sharing a little umbrella and getting soaked. Everleigh's head full of crazy red curls is dripping wet. Hundreds of tiny ringlets still go in a million different directions.

Ben gets driven out of bounds near midfield. Both teams' forwards line up, facing each other on the sideline.

"Line-out," says Hailey. She ignores the rain that soaks her hair. She wears it short with long bangs. One side is shaved right to the skin. "The hooker has to throw the ball straight down the middle."

Hailey is the only one of us who knows anything about rugby. She played junior girls rugby when she was living with her dad in the city last year. Her cousin Liam is on the team playing against ours.

"You'd be great in the line-out, Sarah." Hailey gives Sarah a nudge. Sarah is the tallest girl in grade nine. She's always the star of the All-Native Basketball Tournament.

"Me?" Sarah points to herself. "Are you kidding? That looks like some kind of a war."

"Yeah, sure," Hailey scoffs. "I've seen you out there." She means on the basketball court, where Sarah is all business — knees and elbows. "You're a beast!"

Sarah always has a smile in her eyes and she loves a good laugh. "You got it all wrong." She lifts one eyebrow and shakes her head, trying to look innocent. "I'm all about peace and love."

"One minute!" shouts the ref. "One minute to play."

Ben is thirty metres out from the posts. He's lining up a penalty kick. The crowd is quiet.

"There was a cheap shot in the line-out," Hailey whispers to me. "The kick will give us the win."

The boys' rugby team is the pride of the school and

some of the guys are pretty cocky. They've got team jackets and track suits, and they take a fancy charter bus to travel. Not the old yellow boneshaker we get for girls' volleyball.

Ben focuses on the ball, glances up at the posts and looks down again. He takes three steps forward and boots the ball like he's done it a million times. The ball sails over the crossbar and through the posts. The whistle blasts to end the game. The crowd erupts and our guys mob each other.

Hailey throws Sarah a high-five. Everleigh is bouncing. She throws herself at me for a hug. I stumble and thump into the person behind me. It's old Ms. Oblinski. I almost knock her off her cane.

I reach out to steady Ms. O. "Sorry!" I hold her elbow tight with both hands.

Ms. O is an English teacher. She's grey-haired and looks like she's ready for the retirement home. I'm surprised she's even out here.

"I'm all right," she shrugs.

"Sorry, Ms. O," I repeat.

"I'm fine." She turns and trudges toward the school. She leans on her cane with every step.

The teams shake hands and clap each other off the field. Ben gives a speech to thank the other team for the game. He gives their captain a flat of Gatorade. No one seems to notice the rain falling in a steady cold drizzle.

"Hey, Cuz!" Hailey's cousin Liam steps up to us with his arms open wide. Like all the players, he's soaked to the skin. One of his ears is half clogged with mud and he's got a good-sized nick on the bridge of his nose. A tiny trickle of blood runs down from it.

"Great game." Hailey gives her muddy cousin a full-on bear hug.

"Close one." Liam swipes at the blood with the back of his wrist.

"It looks like a blast!" says Everleigh. "I just love it! You've got a little bit of mud in your ear." She points. "Right there. We'd love to play." She looks at me, Hailey and Sarah. "Right?"

"You bet!" Hailey nods.

Liam is using his baby finger to dig the mud out of his ear as I hear myself say, "We should start our own team."

2 The PLEDGE

As soon as I saw the first player race upfield with the ball, I imagined Everleigh, Hailey, Sarah and myself in rugby gear. I'm the smallest in my class and my nickname is Peanut. But I could still play.

"Yeah!" Everleigh says. "We should play. Peanut is super fast and there's no one tougher than Hailey. She does rodeo, but not barrels, like you'd think. She wrestled a steer last year and almost threw him, too."

"Let's do it," Hailey blurts.

The conversation skids to a stop. We stare at her.

"Call the nut house," Sarah points her index finger to her temple. "We got ourselves some full-fledged crazy girls right here."

Everleigh's electric blue eyes dart back and forth. "Let's do it!"

Hailey throws one arm over my shoulders and the other over Sarah's. "I'm in!" she says.

I can tell Sarah is thinking about it.

We pull into a tight horseshoe. There's a second of silence.

"What are we supposed to do?" Sarah asks. "Some swear-on-our-lives kind of thing? Some crazy spit-in-your-hand pledge thing?"

Hailey locks eyes with Sarah. She makes a loud hawking sound. It's mostly fake, but then she shocks the crap out of all of us. She spits right in her own hand.

Sarah lets her mouth drop open. She gives a huge eye roll like this is the weirdest thing ever. "Really? Like some Friday night bad TV-movie spit pledge?"

Everleigh holds her palm open and gazes at it. "If this means what I think it means, I'll do it. But I'm not spitting unless this is a real, everybody-in, full on pledge."

Hailey gives Everleigh a nod.

Everleigh spits. Half of it dribbles down her chin. She giggles and holds up her palm for proof.

"Oh, crap." Sarah bites her lip. We stare at her. "I guess I've got to follow my girls." Sarah shakes her head. "Crazy-horse, bat-crap, crazy sisters." Sarah holds a palm in front of her and makes the same noisy hawk-up sound that Hailey did. "*Thew!*" she spits.

I know I have to spit next. But part of me is thinking, *you'll be in real trouble if some runaway truck crunches you.* My three best friends are eyeballing me.

"You need me to do the math?" Sarah asks.

"You're next." Hailey points at my hand.

"Just do it," says Everleigh.

My voice is locked in my throat. I take a big breath in and spit. "*P'tew!*" It's just a little spit-spray, but it lands right in my palm.

★★★

Everleigh, Sarah and I all live on the same block, so we always walk home together. At my place, the three of us kick off our wet shoes. My mom, dad and I live in a big cozy log house with a wood fireplace.

"You look like drowned rats." My mom is still in her nursing scrubs. She has a pot of chili on the bubble. The kitchen windows are steamed up and I can see the garlic bread getting crisp in the oven.

"You know what, Mrs. B?" Everleigh can't wait to break the news. She spits out our plans rapid-fire. "We're starting our own rugby team. Junior girls. Sure is warm in here." She fans herself. "The boys have a team and we're going to, too. Getting uniforms, a coach and everything."

"It's true, Mrs. B," Sarah pipes up. She's doing her best sad and sorry impression. "We did it. Committed ourselves to rugby. Full-on mud-wrestling fight for a white rubber ball with no protective gear —"

"Quit whining," Everleigh cuts her off. "You're tougher than all of us." Then she turns back to Mom. "We did a spit-pledge, Mrs. B. Just like you'd see on TV or a kick-ass movie."

Mom catches my eye. She raises both eyebrows. I know the look. She's asking, *Really?*

I nod.

Mom turns and stirs the chili with a wooden spoon. "Should I put out extra plates?" she asks.

"Thanks, Mrs. B," says Everleigh, "but I've got dance." Everleigh is a highland dancer.

"My night to cook," says Sarah, looking at her watch. "World famous Shake 'n Bake. But it smells great. Thanks."

"Rugby is a pretty tough game," says Mom.

"But you're tough. Right, Mrs. B?" says Everleigh. "You played college hockey."

"But that was hockey." Mom purses her lips. "Are there actual rules in rugby?"

"Rugby is the best," says Everleigh. "Liam had mud in his ear. I love that."

Mom shakes a little more chili powder into the pot. "You know me," she says. "I'm okay with almost anything. I guess. But do you girls know what you're getting into?"

Mom is not asking the girls. She's asking me.

"If my friends are in, I'm in too," I say. My friends are my life.

"I think it's a done deal, Mrs. B." Everleigh stretches out one of her curls. She releases it and it springs back.

"Crazy-horse, bat-crap crazy, Mrs. B. But we're all in." Sarah shakes her head like she has surrendered.

"I'm just a bit worried." Mom catches my eye. "What's your dad going to say?"

My dad has always been super protective. When I was little he didn't even want me to head the ball in soccer. "You could get a concussion," he said. And when we had our first elementary floor hockey team he showed up with a helmet. And wanted me to wear it.

"I've got to go," says Everleigh.

"Me too." Sarah checks her watch again.

"Here, girls." Mom opens the oven and the buttery smell of the garlic bread wafts across the room. "Take a slice with you."

3 Big PLANS

Minutes after the girls have left, Dad comes in from work. I open my arms. Dad and I have a routine. He pretends he's going to hug me but instead muscles me into a one-arm headlock. Then he smacks a big kiss on the top of my head. I love Dad's work smell — fresh cut fir and a spicy trace of diesel.

Dad is a logger, built big and thick. He's got muscle that bunches up at the back of his shaved head. There are two big bulges back there at the base of his skull. When Everleigh and I were little, he let us tuck quarters in there. One time we worked a buck seventy-five into what Dad calls his skull muscle.

He shoves me away playfully. "You're all wet, Peanut!"

"I've been watching rugby," I say. "And we're going to start our own team."

Mom gives Dad a peck on the cheek and disappears upstairs.

"Who is?" Dad turns and stirs the chili.

"Me and the girls at school. Sarah, Hailey and Everleigh."

"You're kidding, right?" His eyes are serious.

"Not kidding," I say. "We're serious."

"Rugby?" He drops the spoon on the counter and chili splats on his shirt. "You'll get flattened out there, Maddy."

"Lots of girls play rugby."

"People get their heads torn off!" He throws his hands in the air. "It's a crazy game."

"I just watched an entire game, Dad," I say. "Not one head got torn off."

"Guys get stomped in rugby, Maddy. And it's always the biggest kids who play. You're just not . . ."

"Not what, Dad?" I say. "Not big enough?"

He snatches the spoon and turns back to the chili.

"You always say size doesn't matter." I step next to him.

He stirs the chili. Now he's quiet.

I wonder if I should have challenged him. When he goes silent, I know he's digging his heels in. But I really want to play. Or at least think I do. What I do want, for sure, is the choice.

"You should think about my side of it," I say.

"Is there a teacher on board, to get this thing off the ground?" He bangs the spoon on the side of the pot.

"Not yet."

"You guys know anything about rugby?"

"Hailey does," I say. "She played a whole year in the city."

"Great," he mumbles. "So who's going to coach?"

I shrug. "The boys' coach already said no."

"So, no coach." He stirs the chili so hard a glop hops out of the pot.

"Not yet."

"Just you, Everleigh, Sarah and Hailey?"

"So far."

He taps the spoon on the pot. "Okay."

There's a long moment of me just looking at his clenched jaw. "Okay, what?" I finally say.

"Okay, you can practice with the girls . . . I guess." He turns to face me. "If you even get that far."

★★★

The next morning I hustle up the stairs at the front of the school. It's twenty minutes until the bell. My friends are at our table at the back of the cafeteria.

"I'm making a list," Everleigh says, holding up a sheet of paper. "All the things we need. For the team."

Sarah leans back in her chair, her long legs stretched out a mile in front of her. Hailey is chomping at an apple like she hasn't eaten in a week.

I sit down. I need a couple minutes to finish my homework, an essay outline for Ms. O's English class. I pop my laptop open.

"Here's what we have so far," Everleigh reads. "Number one, we need a coach and a teacher sponsor. Number two," Everleigh stabs her pen onto the list. "Uniforms."

"How much does a bus driver cost?" asks Sarah. "About?"

We live in a little mill town an hour from anywhere. Two hours from anything big enough to be called a real city. We need a bus to get to a game.

"Doesn't the school pay for it?" I'm half listening, half reading my outline. "For the bus, I mean?"

"Good question." Everleigh scribbles the question on her list.

"They should." Hailey tosses her apple core and it clunks into a plastic garbage can.

Everleigh keeps reading. "Equipment." She taps the list with her pen. "But maybe we can use the boys' stuff."

I'm trying to listen while I'm cutting and pasting bits of my outline.

"What are you working on, Peanut?" Sarah leans over and puts her nose in my laptop.

"English," I say. "Essay for Ms. O."

"Uh oh!" Sarah bolts upright in her chair. "Well, you better get it right, sister." She throws me a salute. "Cross the *t*s, dot the *i*s."

"Yeah, yeah." I pretend I'm chill. But the truth is, Ms. O is the world's toughest teacher.

Sarah pokes at the screen. "Who's that?"

There is a photo of a cheerful blonde woman with a warm smile.

"That's Kayla Moleschi," I explain. "Ms. O says we can write about anything that truly inspires us. I found Kayla on YouTube."

"The Canada Sevens player?" Hailey pulls her chair over. "I just saw her interviewed. Moleschi has played in more tournaments than anyone."

"Pretty close." I scroll for the information. "She's tied, second in the world, for most games played on the World Seven-a-side Series."

"Seven-a-side?" asks Everleigh. "What the heck is that?"

"It's a super popular version of rugby. Seven players per side and only two seven-minute halves," Hailey explains. "Canada's women are ranked third in the world, and Kayla has been playing sevens since forever."

"Since 2011," I say.

"And check this out," Sarah reads off the screen. "Kayla is one hundred and sixty centimetres tall. That's like . . . five three?"

"Smallest player on the team," Hailey nods. "But super solid. And tough."

"Her coach nicknamed her Meatball. She's small but mighty," I say. "And no wonder, she's all muscle. Watched a couple videos — killer tackler."

"And a boss offload," says Hailey.

"She's only a bit taller than you, Peanut," says Sarah.

"So what are you saying?"

"You could kick ass, just like Kayla Moleschi."

As soon as I saw Kayla on YouTube I felt a shiver. There was just something about her, the way she talked about rugby, confident but not cocky. It made me believe. Believe in myself. My inner voice said, I can be good at rugby.

"Watch this." I turn the screen so they can all see. It's a twenty-second video of Kayla Moleschi. "I could watch this a million times." I hit play.

It's Canada playing New Zealand. Canada is down 19 to 12, two minutes to play. Canada has the ball way back on their own 22-metre line. The New Zealand defence races up fast. Kayla catches a long high pass and pulls it to her chest.

"Ball in two hands," says Hailey, "so the defence doesn't know if she's going to pass, kick or run."

Kayla steals a glance toward her backline, like she might pass. When the defender slides out just a hair, she explodes through a gap.

"Look at that!" Everleigh slaps the table.

Kayla races five steps then vaults up off the turf. For a couple steps it's like she's running on air! We can feel her energy. Her power. But the sweeper is right on her! Kayla plants a right foot and bursts left with an exploding sidestep. She leaves the defender grabbing thin air.

Everleigh jumps to her feet. "Go, go, go!"

Kayla blasts into high gear with a New Zealander right on her heels. The defender dives, but Kayla is too fast. She outraces everyone.

The commentator has an Australian accent. "This is a beautiful run!" As Kayla races downfield, his voice gets louder. He's yelling, "Moleschi takes it to the house!"

Kayla dashes all the way across the goal line, slides in under the posts, touches down and rests her head on the ball. It's a seventy-metre score!

"Holy crap!" Sarah lets her mouth hang open a second.

Everleigh looks stunned. "Amazing!"

"I know, right?" I say. "You should see it in slow-mo. If Ms. O doesn't think that's inspirational, nothing is."

"You know what I'm going to do?" Hailey stands up and throws her school bag over one shoulder. "I'm going to set it up with Mr. Sharma."

"Set what up?" asks Everleigh.

"A meeting. The whole team, so we can meet with him." Mr. Sharma is the principal, always in a jacket and tie. Not that approachable a guy.

"The whole team?" Sarah uses her index finger to count us. "One, two, three, four. I count four."

4 Shot DOWN

At lunch the four of us file into Mr. Sharma's big conference room. He's sitting at the head of a massive glass-top table. "Come on in, ladies." He gestures to the chairs. "Have a seat."

My seat turns out to be right next to his. I tuck one foot under my butt so I don't get swallowed by the big armchair. The room is way too warm. Stuffy. I get a whiff of stale coffee. For a second it seems like the air is too thick to breathe.

"I've invited Mrs. Levens," he says. "Makes sense to have our athletic director on board."

Mrs. Levens struts into the room right on cue. "Morning, girls." Her tone is frigid. She picks an invisible something off her shoulder and says, "I've got another meeting at twelve-thirty." She drops a big Ziploc bag of chopped vegetables on the table. That's all she ever eats. Red pepper, carrots and turnip.

Who eats raw turnip?

"I can give you my best ten minutes." She drops into a chair and rakes her eyes across the bunch of us.

Mr. Sharma takes a moment to adjust his tie and make sure it's cinched up tight around his neck. He doesn't say anything. There's a bit of awkward silence and it seems like we should say something. I thought Hailey would take the lead, but she's just looking down at the mock-up drawing of our team jersey. Her bangs hide her eyes. Everleigh is chewing her thumbnail. Sarah glances across the table at me.

"It's about the girls' rugby team." I try to sit tall in my chair. "Hailey talked to you about it, Mr. Sharma?"

Hailey peeks out from under her bangs and nods, but misses her cue to say something. Everleigh is bug-eyed, still gnawing her thumb.

This is not like us. Even Sarah seems a bit freaked. And why am I talking? I'm not even sure I'd make the team.

Mr. Sharma looks down the table to Mrs. Levens.

"Heard all about it." Mrs. Levens looks at her watch. "And before we get started dreaming about fancy new uniforms," she points a finger at Hailey's drawing, "I've got to tell you. Field time? It's booked. Completely. Monday, Wednesday and Friday is boys' rugby. Tuesday and Thursday intramurals. And the inside skinny on funding? There is none. All the team sport money was allocated back in September." She leans back in her chair.

I've never seen this side of her. As our volleyball coach she's great. Always encouraging, smiling.

"All of it?" I ask. "The funding?"

"Every nickel." Mrs. Levens looks out the window. Her lips are pressed so tight it looks like she'll never smile again.

"That's policy, the way we do it every year," says Mr. Sharma. He slides his tie, right, left and back to centre. "Sorry, ladies, but is rugby really your thing?"

"It is," Sarah leans forward, "and I think we'd be good at it."

Everleigh is still speechless. She looks back and forth from Mrs. Levens to Mr. Sharma.

"There's a lot of girls' teams that —" Hailey starts, but Mrs. Levens cuts her off.

"Our volleyball team kicked butt this season. Right, girls?" She looks at me, at Sarah then at Everleigh.

I nod.

"So why don't you, Hailey, join our squad?" She tries a smile. "Get everybody on board for this year's volleyball championship. Everyone wants to be on a winning team. And a volleyball championship season will be better for the school's sports standings than girls playing rugby."

"We're talking about rugby," Hailey pokes a finger onto the table. "It's not just for guys. Lots of girls play rugby. All over the province —"

"All it takes is one broken finger and your volleyball season is over," interrupts Mrs. Levens.

"I played a whole season." Hailey holds up all ten fingers. "And look at this, I never —"

"Sorry." Mrs. Levens stands up with a long skinny carrot in hand. She snaps off a loud bite. "Maybe try again in September." She gives Mr. Sharma a curt salute and walks out.

It seems like rugby is over before it can even start. I slump back into my chair.

Hailey slides the jersey drawing toward Mr. Sharma. "This is what we were thinking," she mutters.

"There's a handful of soccer uniforms in the old equipment room," he says. He touches an index finger to his forehead. "A bin marked 2010, I think." Mr. Sharma carefully places both palms on the table. "But I may have what you girls are looking for."

"Yeah?" Everleigh leans across the table. "What is it, Mr. Sharma?"

"There's a trust fund we could access." Mr. Sharma puts on a dramatic and very cheesy whisper. "Funds have been sitting unused for years. You might be just the ladies. I'd love to reignite this thing."

"What?" Everleigh is gnawing her thumb again.

Mr. Sharma puts his hands in prayer position. "It's the old cheerleaders' trust fund," he says. "What do you ladies think about cheerleading?"

★★★

After school, Sarah, Everleigh and I meet at Simply Smoothies. It's a bright little place with oversize windows. We sit knee to knee at our window table with three tall smoothies, waiting for Hailey. Outside, rain patters for the third day in a row. It seems like the rugby idea has sunk. I might be a little sketched about my size, but I didn't even get a chance to try.

"Skirts and pompoms!" Everleigh jabs her straw into her thick raspberry smoothie. "Can you believe it?"

"I'd like to see *him* with a skirt and pompoms," snorts Sarah.

I get a vision of Mr. Sharma I don't want to see. "Ew!" I say.

Everleigh points two fingers at her temple. "Now how am I ever going to un-see that?"

"Sorry," Sarah says. She holds her palms up. "Didn't mean to put you off."

"What put me off," says Everleigh, "was Levens. Why so witchy? I mean, really."

"Yeah," Sarah tries to imitate Mrs. Levens. "'One broken finger and your season is over.'"

I'm guessing Mrs. Levens is a bit like my dad. Overprotective. It's like her volleyball players are the most precious things in the world. "It's not even volleyball season." I drag my straw on the surface of my mango smoothie and make slurping sounds.

Shot Down

"People just don't get girls' rugby." Everleigh stirs her drink with a long metal spoon. It *tic, tic, tics* against the glass. "If guys can play, we can too."

The tiny bell above the door *tink-tinks* and Hailey steps in out of the rain. She's dripping wet, bangs flat and glued with water over one eye. But she's beaming a smile and holding a rugby ball in each hand.

"I'm happy to announce," she takes a deep bow, "that the first Stampeders girls' rugby practice will take place Thursday at lunch."

"Who's the coach?" asks Everleigh.

Hailey slaps the balls on the table. "You're looking at her!"

5 FAIL

Thursday at lunch we huddle together on the small field behind the school. It's an overgrown patch of ground that used to be a baseball diamond. The rain has stopped but there's a chilly breeze. There are ten of us, Grade Nine and Ten girls, in shorts, T-shirts and runners. I wish I'd worn another layer.

I've got my arms wrapped tight around myself. I'm shivering, and wondering if I should actually be here. Am I really cut out for rugby? I look around. I'm going up against some of the toughest girls in school.

Lily Nguyen is bouncing on her toes, shadow boxing. Maybe she's trying to stay warm. Maybe she's showing off. She's a featherweight in the local boxing club. Her nickname is Lightning Lily.

Tara Leota is in a muscle shirt. Really? Like it's not cold as heck out here? She plays hockey in the boys' league. And she has biceps. Not quite Kayla Moleschi biceps, but it's clear she's been hitting the gym.

Fail

Hailey comes trotting across the field with her two rugby balls and a handful of field markers. "Hey, guys!" She stops in front of our ragtag group. "We've got about forty minutes. Let's do a lap to warm up."

Hailey leads, we follow. The sideline is flooded with puddles. When a splash of water hits my thigh I'm shocked at how cold it is. I trot next to Bobbi Mason, the biggest girl in the group. I need to hustle to keep up with them.

This isn't at all like volleyball. It's cold, it's wet and I feel like I'm about to get slaughtered.

"Okay, get into three lines of three," yells Hailey. She asks Sarah to step forward. They demonstrate a little series of passing and catching. "Use a soft pass," says Hailey. "Keep your hands up to give your partner a target. In your threes, just trot and pass, across the field and back."

Ava Royal is in my group. She kind of prances as she jogs, arms swinging side to side. I toss her a pass, a bit high, straight at her head. She shrieks and bats the ball to the ground.

"Cripes, Maddy," she whines. "Are you trying to kill me?"

Sarah is a great basketball player but she's not getting the drill. She lags behind, then throws a long forward pass.

"Backward passes," says Hailey. "Only pass backward in rugby."

"Then how do we get anywhere?" Sarah asks. "To go forward, pass backward?" She mutters, "One crazy-ass game."

Tara Leota throws a hard pass that goes through Lily Nguyen's hands and clonks her in the forehead.

"You idiot!" Lily grabs ahold of Tara's shirt. It looks like we're going to have a fist fight ten minutes into our first practice.

Hailey races over and gets in between the two of them. "Let's change it up!" Hailey's voice is an octave higher than usual. I can hear the stress in her voice. She gives us a quick talk about tackling. It takes her a few minutes to set us up for a one-on-one tackle drill. We've got a narrow grid for the runner to get past the tackler.

"Let's just see how we do," says Hailey.

Sarah starts. She has the ball in hand and lopes toward Tara. Tara rushes forward and throws herself shoulder first, knees tucked into her belly, like a cannonball. Sarah braces for the hit. It knocks her flat.

"No, no, no!" Hailey grabs a fistful of her own hair. "We have to wrap. Wrap with our arms."

For a few seconds Sarah has lost her breath. She has her hands on her knees and is gasping.

"Sorry about that," Tara whispers.

Sarah drops a hand on Tara's shoulder, still breathing hard. "No problem. Nice hit."

I'm not sure if Hailey's practice is a disaster, or if this is just how rugby practice is supposed to go.

Fail

I'm up next. I have to get past Lily Nguyen. *Great*, I think. It's not just that she spends her spare time punching people. It's her name, Lightning Lily.

I take off at a bit of a trot, holding the ball out front like a stinky bag of garbage. Before I can even think about how I can try to sneak past, Lily launches herself at me. She hits me with a rock-solid shoulder, full force, just above the knees. Her arms clamp around, and she drives me into the ground. *Bam!*

"Perfect!" says Hailey. "Textbook tackle."

My shoulder is throbbing where I crashed into the ground.

"You okay, Maddy?" Lily helps me up.

"Yeah," I say. "I'm good." Truth is, my shoulder feels like it's on fire. I raise my arm a bit and pain jolts all the way down to my elbow.

"You okay, Peanut?" Hailey rubs a hand on my shoulder.

"I'm good." I try to smile, and I roll my shoulder a bit, like it's nothing. But there's a red-hot throb going on. My inner voice is yelling at me, *are you really going to play rugby, Maddy? Your nickname is Peanut for a reason!*

"We're going to ease up a little before someone gets killed," Hailey says. "Let's try some unopposed. Like a game but no defence. The nine of you run and pass the ball down the field. When I shout 'tackle,' go to ground. The nearest player picks up and we play on. Okay?"

There are a lot of puzzled looks. I don't get it, but I'll do what everyone else does. The fire in my shoulder has calmed to a dull ache.

"And you'll say 'tackle'?" Tara clarifies.

"Yeah, then you pretend you get tackled."

"Do we have positions?" asks Everleigh.

"Not yet." Hailey grabs another little fistful of her hair.

I can tell she's rattled. This practice isn't going like she planned.

"Just . . . just run as a pack," Hailey says.

It doesn't make sense to me. But I'll see what happens.

"Okay?" Hailey throws a ball to Sarah. "You lead."

Sarah takes off downfield. She passes to Everleigh. Everleigh passes to Ava, who actually catches. Ava prances on the spot, not sure what to do.

"Keep going!" Hailey yells.

Bobbi catches the pass from Ava.

"Keep going," yells Hailey again. "This is good."

Bobbi passes to Tara.

"Nice," calls Hailey, "now take a tackle."

Tara falls to the ground. So does Everleigh. Then Ava. I'm confused. Everyone falls like they've been shot! So I do too.

We lie there and look up at Hailey. She has her hands on her hips and her head down. Then she looks up, eyes wide, in total disbelief. Then both fists dig into her hair.

"Crap," she spits. "Holy crap!" And she laughs.

What's so funny? I wonder.

"Maybe we weren't all supposed to fall down," Sarah suggests.

Now that I think about it, everyone falling down at once . . . kind of weird.

"Maybe just the ball carrier was supposed to fall down," Sarah says. "Right?"

The school bell rings.

"Saved!" yells Hailey and looks up at the sky. "Saved by the bell."

Most of the girls head for the school. Hailey's head is down, hands on her hips, again.

"You okay?" I ask.

She starts walking. She bends to pick up the field markers. "I thought I could do it, Peanut."

I see the frustration in her eyes.

"I thought it was pretty good," I lie.

"I'm a player." Hailey glances at me. "Not a coach. We need a real coach, Peanut."

6 ONE-ON-ONE

By Sunday I've thought about it from a lot of different angles. My fear of being the shrimp on the field. My shoulder is almost back to normal. I can lift it with no pain, do a few push-ups. No problem. I can take it, I keep telling myself. A few hits, no big deal.

The Horvats are over for dinner. The juicy smell of Mom's roast beef wafts all through the house. In the living room, Mr. Horvat eases his bulk onto the couch. Tiny Mrs. Horvat perches on the edge of the piano stool like a bird. The twins, six-year-old Emma and Anna, sit in their usual spot on the love seat. The Horvats have been coming for Sunday dinners once a month since I was in diapers.

Mom balances a tray of nibbles in each hand. Dad follows with glasses of wine.

I'm in the kitchen. Mom has asked me to take the pies out of the oven.

Ben is in jeans and a T-shirt. He's leaning against the counter. Lots of girls would be thrilled to have Ben

Horvat over for dinner. But Ben and I have known each other forever.

"You guys had your first practice," he says. "How'd it go?"

I'm not sure why he's asking. He could be setting me up to look dumb. He does that sometimes.

"Yep." I slide the first pie onto the stovetop. "It was pretty good."

"Many girls show up?"

"Ten of us," I say. "Okay, I guess, for the first practice."

"That's not bad."

I guess he's just curious. Mostly we get along really well. When Ben turned thirteen he was suddenly in high school. Cute, sporty and popular. When I got up there I thought he might shun me, but just the opposite. On my first day, he helped me find the locker room for gym class.

"Who's coming out?" he asks.

I take the oven mitts off and stack them one on top of the other. "Me, Hailey, Sarah and Everleigh. Bobbi Mason . . . and Lily Nguyen."

"Lightning Lily!" Ben slaps the counter. "Lily Nguyen is coming out for rugby." Ben looks at me wide-eyed. "Awesome! She could play on our team."

"But she's on our team, not with you bozos."

"She'd be a killer flanker."

"Flanker?"

"Yeah, the first two players to break off the scrum are the flankers. They make a million tackles."

"She's solid all right. I had to do a one-on-one drill with her," I explain. "One tackle and she nearly killed me."

"Hailey teach you a straight arm?"

"A what?"

"Straight arm?" He holds his palm out toward me. "Nope."

He pulls open the door to go outside. "Come on." He waves for me to follow. We take the steps into the backyard. "Hang on a sec." Ben trots over to the driveway and pops their car door open. When he jogs back, he's tossing a rugby ball from hand to hand.

"Straight arm." He tucks the ball under one arm. "For strong, fast players like Lightning Lily Nguyen. Use a straight arm." He holds his palm straight out at me. "It's what you need, Nutty."

Ben calls me Nutty sometimes. He's the only one, and I like it. It's his short form for Peanut.

"We'll slow it right down," he says. "Just a jog. You come and tackle me."

"Just like that," I say. "You want me to tackle you." I'm stalling, thinking about a couple things. Can I tackle him? And how wet is the grass? It rained this morning. The sun is out now, but I can't let him think I'm worried about getting a bit wet.

"You know how, right?"

"Of course." Now I need to prove that I know what I'm doing. "I'm going to hit you low, shoulder to thigh." I'm reciting what I watched on YouTube. "Wrap with my arms, lock my hands together, drive my legs and dump you into the turf, Captain Horvat."

"Whoa!" He pops his eyes wide, sticks a fist between his teeth, and fakes like he's scared. "Okay . . . I guess." He turns his back to me and jogs away.

He's a perfect target!

I jog toward him. My plan is to move in slowly, then catch him off guard. Ben keeps trotting toward the back fence. We have a big yard that slopes a bit downhill. The downhill will give me an advantage on the final burst.

"Are you going to do it?" Ben calls back to me over his shoulder.

"Just keep going." I'm a few feet behind. He has his back to me. It's my chance! I dash the last couple steps and shoot for his legs. He twists his upper body to face me. Just before contact I feel the pressure of his palm on my shoulder. Not hard. Just enough that I can't reach him. I skid to a stop, knees down, in the grass.

It's wetter than I thought. And cold. I pop up to my feet and look at the wet grass stains on my knees.

"It's a straight arm, or a fend." Ben is jogging on the spot. "Perfectly legal if you don't aim for the guy's face or try to intentionally injure."

I really thought I had him. It's like his straight arm came out of nowhere.

"Okay, I get it." I brush at the wet knees of my jeans. "Give me another shot."

"Sure." He turns his back to me again and jogs away.

This time I know what's coming. I'll go lower. Get under the straight arm.

Ben makes a long arcing turn and heads back toward the house. I move up right behind him and maintain a trot so we're just a couple metres apart. I need to time it perfectly. I crouch low in my run. I drive with my legs and project myself straight at his calves.

Somehow he swivels himself around. I'm airborne when I feel his hand on top of my head, shoving me down. I hit the ground face-first. Arms empty. I get a taste of cut grass. I swipe a quick hand across my lips.

"Great technique, Nutty," Ben says. "It's easy for me because I know you're coming at me." He tosses me the ball. "You try. Tuck the ball under one arm, use the other to fend me off, hand open. Just shove me away when I move in for the tackle."

I trot off toward the back fence, ready for him.

Ben comes in high, at half speed. I've got my arm bent at the elbow, and I give him a solid shove, middle of the chest. He stumbles back a couple steps.

"Beauty," he says. "You've got it. I'll try coming in a little lower."

This time he's aimed at my waist. I get a hand on his shoulder and try to jam him to the ground. I'm surprised how muscled he feels. Solid. He staggers a step and falls to one knee.

"Good one, Nutty!"

I know what to do next. I pick up the pace. I'm pumped.

He comes at me fast, behind me, from a tough angle. I twist around but I'm late. My straight arm skids over his back. He gets his arms around my waist, a shoulder behind my butt. His weight drives me into the lawn.

"Crap!" I laugh. "Thought I had you."

"Sorry, Nutty. That was more tackle than we needed," he says.

"Hey, Maddy!" It's Emma and Anna, calling from the back deck. "Will you guys stop fighting and come play a game with us?"

Ben hops up, offers me a hand and pulls me to my feet. "You're a natural," he says. "You'll rock at rugby, Nutty."

"Maaaddyyy," calls Anna.

"I'll be right in," I call back to the girls. I look at Ben. "That was good. I can't wait to try it out."

"No problem." Ben is throwing the ball hand to hand.

I start heading inside but stop. "Do you want to coach us? The girls?" I blurt.

"What do you mean?"

"Just try it out?" I ask. "I can tell, you'd be a great coach."

"Do you think?" He throws me a long arcing pass.

"I'm serious," I say. "You'd be awesome."

"I can try." He one-hand catches my pass. "Let me know when."

7 Cop OUTS

I share a locker with Sarah. Right next to us, Everleigh and Hailey share. First thing the next morning, the topic of conversation is Ben Horvat coaching our team.

"That's so cool," says Everleigh.

"Did he say anything about gear?" asks Hailey. "Can we use the guys' stuff?"

"I think Ben will rock," says Everleigh.

"One thing for sure," I say, "we need to get a few more girls out."

"Totally." Hailey flings her binder into her bag. "So how about we each recruit one player?"

"Easy," says Everleigh.

"One each would put us up to fourteen," says Sarah.

"No problem." Hailey thumps her locker door shut. She and Everleigh turn and head toward their class. Sarah and I go in the opposite direction.

"I heard Charlotte Johnny is talking about it," I say.

"She'd be great." Sarah nods. Charlotte is a run-and-gun player on Sarah's basketball team.

"Let's ask her." Sarah points with her chin toward Charlotte's locker.

Charlotte is checking herself in the little mirror on her locker door.

"Hey, gorgeous," Sarah holds out a fist to Charlotte. Charlotte bumps it. "Word on the street is," says Sarah, "I might be getting another sister out on the rugby field."

"I heard you guys are practicing," says Charlotte. "Sounds intense."

"You'd be great," I say. "Want to play?"

"I would." She flips her jet-black hair over one shoulder. "And I was really thinking about it, but I have to work after school. At Mom's shop."

"Maybe take a day off?" suggests Sarah.

"I want to be a carpenter, you know. So it's what I need to do," Charlotte shrugs. "And I need the money. Sorry."

In Math class I sit down right next to Julie Sager. She used to play elementary floor hockey with me and she wasn't bad. So I think, *what the heck, I'll ask her.*

Mr. Tanaka is sitting on the front of his desk, laptop on his thighs. He peeks over stylish glasses, then back at his keyboard. He's totally focused on attendance.

"Julie," I whisper.

She drags her gaze away from her phone, just long enough to glance at me.

"What are you doing Wednesday at lunch?" I ask.

"Why?"

"Want to join rugby?" I use a hushed tone. "I remember you rocked in floor hockey back —"

She cuts me off. "You're joking, right?" Her face goes sour.

My heart sinks.

"I don't play sports anymore," she hisses. She rolls her eyes at me.

At lunch, back in the cafeteria, Everleigh and Hailey both look bummed.

"I tried," says Everleigh. "Everyone has heard about the practice. They say 'yeah, awesome, you guys are great.' But then I get the excuses. One right after the other. Emma Wu said 'yeah, it looks like fun, but there's no future in girls' sports. Especially rugby!' I'm like . . . what?"

Sarah shuffles in the door. She drops backward in her chair and lets her arms hang over the backrest. "I might have set a new record," she says, "for most lame excuses. I've heard it all. 'I've got work, too much homework, after school chores, I'm not tough enough.'"

"Kayla Obi was going to play," says Hailey. "I almost talked her into it, but she's all about tutoring. 'Can't miss, got to be on the honour roll.' Scarlet Tam says it looks like fun, but she has to babysit her brothers."

I don't have the heart to mention Julie Sager. "I can talk to Parm and Preet," I offer. "I'll see them in English." Parm and Preet are twins, both excellent soccer players.

"Anyone get a teacher sponsor?" I ask.

"Nope," says Hailey.

Sarah shakes her head.

"Well how about some good news?" says Everleigh. "Guess what."

"What?"

"I'm starting a GoFundMe page."

"What's the title?" Sarah asks. "Toonies to Tackle?"

"Give Girls a Chance," says Everleigh. "What do you think?"

"Pretty good, Ev," says Hailey.

"I like it." Sarah nods.

"How much are we looking for?" I ask.

"Five grand." Everleigh checks the notes on her phone. "Half of that is uniforms, then there's travel costs, balls, tackle bags, med kit."

"GoFundMe! I love it." Hailey thumps Everleigh on the back. "Have you got a good cover photo?"

"Video!" Everleigh claps her hands. "And you're going to be in it! All of you."

Sarah pushes her chair away, stands and strikes a model pose. One hand is on her hip, one hand combs through her hair. "My chance to be famous."

"It'll be a question and answer," says Everleigh.

"The question: why should girls play rugby? Hailey, you're up first and you say, 'to show our power, our strength.' Then the camera is on you, Sarah. You say, 'we can do anything boys can do.' Maddy, you say, 'passion, discipline, respect.'"

"Ev, you really thought it through," I say.

"I have," she says. "Then the camera goes back to you, Hailey, and you explain that rugby has a position for everyone, big, small, thin, round."

"I love it!" Hailey gives Everleigh another thump.

"You're a rock star!" Sarah points two finger-guns at her.

Everleigh points a finger-gun back. "We film tonight!"

I throw my bag over one shoulder. "Going to see dear Ms. O." We're getting our weekly vocab quiz, and I need a couple extra minutes to review.

"Perfect!" Sarah gives me a thumbs-up. "I'll bet she wants to be our sponsor."

"Ask her," says Everleigh. "You never know."

"Ms. O?" I ask. "Really? She's like a hundred years old."

When I slip into the classroom, Ms. O is writing on the blackboard. She's the only teacher who still uses chalk. There are always big smudges of chalk on her track pants.

Ms. O wears old-school golf shirts with the collars popped, and runners. She's about my height. Rumour is that a hundred years ago, she was a gym teacher. Her cane, like always, is tight in her left hand.

"Hi, Ms. O." I sit at my desk in the front row.

"Good afternoon, Madison," she sings. She keeps clacking her chalk on the board.

She seems to be in a good mood. I think, *what if I just ask her?* I realize I'm chewing the inside of my cheek.

"Ms. O, I have a question." She probably thinks it's about the quiz. "We're wondering," my voice is shaky, "if you'd maybe consider being our teacher sponsor." I start to sweat. "For the rugby team."

Ms. O turns from the blackboard and drops the chalk in her pocket. She puts both hands on the top of her cane, leans forward and digs her eyes into me.

I wonder if I've made her mad.

"I heard about the girls' rugby." She looks past me, out the window. "It's quite surprising. You girls wanting to play."

"I was just —"

She cuts me off. "What is it you like about rugby, Madison?" she asks, still gazing out the window.

She's caught me off guard. The sweat beads on my forehead. Then I remember my lines for the GoFundMe video. "Discipline," I say. "Rugby is about discipline and respect."

She snaps her eyes in my direction. It's like she's looking at me for the first time. Assessing me.

"You've thought about it, haven't you?"

"Yep," I lie.

She looks past me again, out the window. Outside, the rain comes down in sheets. "I'd have to travel on the bus?" she asks.

"I guess," I say. "Yeah."

"Sounds like a big adventure for an old nag like me." There's something sad in her voice. "I'm waiting for a hip operation, you know."

"Oh."

"And my arthritis." She holds up her hand. "It's a real pain in the butt."

"Just thought I'd ask." I shrink into my desk. "Sorry."

She turns back to the board and the chalk *tick, tick, ticks*.

I exhale and wipe the sweat off my forehead. I can tell the girls I tried.

8 JERKS

Wednesday at lunch we're on the sideline waiting for Ben. The skies are finally blue after days of heavy rain. The sun is warm but the field is mostly mud. There are eleven of us. Lacy Barker, known as Lacy Darker, the school loner, hovers on the edge of the group. Her skin is so white I wonder if it's ever seen the sun. She has her black hoodie up over her dyed-black hair and heavy eyeliner.

"Hi, Lacy." I wave although she's only feet away.

"Hi," she nods.

I think it's the first time I've ever spoken to her.

I'm stressed about Ben coaching. Will he single me out somehow? Call me Nutty? I chew the inside of my cheek. I feel my heart thump. What's he going to be like surrounded by girls?

The sun has brought lots of kids outdoors. There's a bunch of guys on the bleachers wearing hockey jackets. One of them is Lyle Fiss. He's a loudmouth with a see-through moustache. His sidekicks sit on either side of him.

Lyle's right-hand man, Ali Chopra, has the collar of

his jacket up. Like always, his hair is stiff with product. Tyson O'Brian has a military buzz cut and a face scarred with acne. He's the school's best definition of a hallway bully. He peels off his jacket for everyone to get a look at his muscle shirt. Then he flexes an arm to admire his bulging bicep.

Ben comes out the back exit of the school. His dri-fit T-shirt is tight across his chest and shoulders. He runs a hand over his new haircut. It's short at the sides with just the right amount of messy on top.

"Come on in, ladies," he calls to us. "Take a knee."

Hailey drops one knee on the ground, keeps the other knee raised to rest a forearm on. We all take a knee and form a semicircle around Ben. I'm surprised how cold the ground is.

"Perfect," he says.

"All kneel for King Horvat," Sarah whispers.

Ben spins a ball on his middle finger like some guys spin a basketball.

"How do you do that?" asks Ava Royal.

"Practice," says Ben. "Lots of practice."

Sarah looks over at me with a raised eyebrow.

I feel like I'm somehow responsible for Ben. I wish he'd stop showing off.

Ben throws the ball straight up overhead in a tight spin. It flies up ten feet and drops, and he catches it behind his back.

"Wow," says Ava. "That's awesome."

Ben smiles and does it again.

"What is this?" Lyle calls from his perch on the bleachers. "A ticket to the Ben Horvat show?"

Ben glares at him. "Everybody get a partner," he says to us.

I wish the hockey guys weren't watching. It feels like we're onstage. Lily Nguyen and I are partners. Ben demonstrates how to pass and catch. We try it. First walking, then jogging.

He calls us back in. "Good job." It seems like Ben is taking his coach role very seriously.

"When are we going to see some action?" Lyle hollers. There are more people on the bleachers now. The sun has brought half the school out.

"Let's see some hits!" yells Tyson.

Ben ignores him. Tara Leota gives him the finger.

"There's a gutsy one!" calls Ali.

"Hey!" hollers Lyle. His face goes dark and he punches his fist in the air, middle finger straight up.

"Couple things to think about when you tackle." Ben is struggling to keep his cool. His face is flushed, his jaw muscles flexing. "A tackle has to be below the shoulders," he says. "Wrap with your arms. Keep your head behind. Can someone help me demo?"

"Sure." Ava tugs her T-shirt down and prances forward.

Ben is on one knee. Ava is standing right next to him. "Like this," he demonstrates as he speaks.

"Shoulder to quad, head behind, wrap with the arms and drive with your legs." As Ava is falling to the ground he says, "keep your arms locked tight."

They both land easily on the ground.

"Always keep your head behind for protection," Ben says. He's all business. I have to give him credit.

"Whoa," calls Lyle. "Only way Horvat can get a girl."

The bleachers are nearly full now. The crowd laughs. Ben ignores them. He hops to his feet and offers Ava a hand up.

Ben gets us to form a circle with Hailey in the middle. "What I want you to do," he says to Hailey, "is make as many tackles as you can in one minute. Girls on the outside just keep jogging and wait for Hailey's tackle."

I roll my shoulders and look at the other girls. I feel smaller than usual.

"Go!" Ben chirps his whistle.

Hailey tackles Bobbi Mason. They hit the ground with a thump.

"Boom!" yells Lyle. "Lights, camera, action!"

The bleacher gang whistles and claps.

Hailey gives me a nod and comes at me. She hits me, shoulder into my upper legs. I'm not ready for her power and my head whiplashes. Hailey's full weight comes down like a ton of bricks on top of me. There's a pain in my knee, and the cold mud is a shock.

"Crack the peanut," yells Tyson.

"Peanut butter," shouts Ali.

"*Boom, boom!*" Lyle adds. "Out go the lights."

They laugh.

I haul myself up, red-faced and mad. I spit.

When it's my turn to be in the middle I bounce a couple times on my toes, then aim at Lacy. I hit her with my shoulder, arms tight around her knees. We hit the ground and slide across the wet grass.

"Good tackle," Lacy smiles. "This is cool."

Next I target Sarah. I hit her a bit high. Sarah leans forward to shrug me off, but I've got a good grip. I pull her down on top of me.

The bleacher crowd whistles and whoops.

"We got some skin!" shouts Ali.

I realize what I've done. I've pulled Sarah's shirt halfway over her head. Her ribs and the back of her sports bra are slick with mud.

Lyle yells again, "Horvat, you suck at coaching almost as much as you suck at playing."

Ben slams a rugby ball to the ground. He marches straight toward Lyle.

My hand flies to my mouth. *What's he doing!*

9 SHOWDOWN

Ben stomps up the first steps of the bleachers, his hands knotted into fists. Lyle stands and strips off his jacket.

A voice booms from the back of the school. "Horvat! Fiss!"

"Levens to the rescue," says Sarah.

Mrs. Levens marches straight toward the bleachers. "Get over here, Horvat!"

Ben is just a few feet from Lyle. "This ain't over," he hisses. He turns and comes down, two steps at a time.

"Fiss," Mrs. Levens calls, "I'll see you in the office." She shouts at the rest of the crowd, "Show's over."

The crowd goes dead quiet. Most of them leave the bleachers and head for the school.

I watch Mrs. Levens lecture Ben on the sideline.

"I think I've got mud in my armpit," Sarah says, reaching up under her shirt. "Is that part of the game? Getting mud where it's never been before?"

Mrs. Levens strides over to us as Ben heads back inside.

"You know you need a certified coach for a school team?" She lets the message sink in. "Any of you girls thinking the volleyball team might be a better option than this . . . " she frowns, "this mud war?"

"This is rugby." Hailey picks a little piece of grass off her lip. "We're playing rugby, Mrs. Levens." She turns her head and spits.

Mrs. Levens folds her arms high up on her chest. She turns her head, and she spits a little something too.

Sarah whispers in my ear, "Showdown."

"If there's one thing I know about rugby," says Mrs. Levens, "it's that you've got to be fit." She chirps her whistle and points. "Everybody on the goal line!"

"Are you our new coach?" Everleigh asks.

The bunch of us trot over and line up along the goal line. I think I know what she has in mind.

"Are you our new coach?" Everleigh asks again.

"Wind sprints," Mrs. Levens calls out. "Sprint to centre, jog back."

She tweets her whistle and we charge to centre. I'm pretty fast, but my knee is bugging me. We turn around and jog back.

"Again." Mrs. Levens blasts the whistle. "And give me ten push-ups when you get back here!"

For the next ten minutes she runs us. We do sprints, push-ups and more sprints. Back and forth, until I'm gasping, totally out of gas. I ease to the ground and muscle out a couple shaky push-ups.

Mrs. Levens opens her Ziploc bag, pulls out a wedge of turnip and casually takes a nip. "Anybody want to head into the gym?"

All of us are sucking big gulps of air. We're mud-caked from push-ups. Lacy and Ava have their hands on their knees, gasping.

The gym sounds warm and dry. But my inner voice says, *don't give in.*

"No, thanks," Hailey pants. "We're sticking with rugby." Hailey turns and starts jogging down the sideline. "Come on, girls," she calls over her shoulder. "Cool-down lap."

One by one we follow her.

I can feel Mrs. Levens's eyes burning into my back, but I keep jogging, girls on either side of me.

"You need fifteen players!" Mrs. Levens barks at us. "I see eleven." She stomps back to the school.

When we get to the far end of the field Hailey stops us. "Hold up," she says. "I know how we can keep this team alive. Next practice, we go to Rotary Park."

"But we need a certified coach for a school team," says Everleigh.

Hailey smirks. "Maybe we're not a school team. Maybe we're just a bunch of girls with a rugby ball."

10 Just a Bunch of Girls WITH A BALL

A couple days later we've got Rotary Park all to ourselves. The park gets used mostly on weekends for little kid soccer. Everleigh is next to me, counting the number of players.

"How many?"

"Twelve," she says. "Not bad!"

"How's the GoFundMe?" asks Tara Leota.

"Pretty quiet." Everleigh shrugs.

"I'll get my parents to donate," says Bobbi Mason. She's helping Hailey lay out a couple lines of field markers.

"We'll use half a field," says Hailey. She hands each of us a strip of fabric. "Tuck these in your shorts at the hip," she says. "Let a foot or so hang out."

Hannah Alec is out for her first practice. She's solid and built low to the ground. Won a silver medal at the Zones wrestling. "What are they for?" she asks.

"Flag rugby," says Hailey.

Hannah tucks the strips in her waistband so they hang over each hip.

Flag rugby, I think. Great. Maybe no hitting today. I've been trying to ignore my knee but it's been sore since last practice.

I should probably have taken today off. But when Hailey said we had practice, I said I'd be there. I don't want the team to lose momentum.

"Heads up." Tara uses her thumb to point toward the park entrance.

Ms. O is walking our way. An old black lab walks at her side.

"Dog looks older than Ms. O," Sarah whispers.

Ms. O shuffles through the entrance and straight toward the knot of us. She's in her usual uniform — track pants and golf shirt. But she's also wearing an old-school ball cap. I've never seen her in a ball cap.

"Does the school know you're having rugby practice?" she asks. The dog stands right next to her on his old, stick-like legs.

Hailey tosses a ball from hand to hand and tries to smile. "We're not a school team . . . " she stammers. I can tell she doesn't have a good answer.

"Just a bunch of friends," says Lily Nguyen. "Playing a bit of touch . . . is all."

Ms. O slides her glasses down her nose and peers over them for a better look. First she eyeballs Lily, then Hailey. "And City Hall?" she asks. "Do they know you're on their field?"

"My dad works for City Hall," says Ava. "I'll let him know."

Ms. O doesn't respond. She surveys the group of us. For a long moment she lets the silence sink in.

I shift from one foot to the other. Maybe we're too cheeky. Maybe she's memorizing who's here. Making a mental list, to get us in trouble.

Finally she gives the dog's leash a gentle tug. "Come on, Charles." She shuffles toward the sidewalk. The old dog totters next to her.

"Good luck, then, girls," she calls over her shoulder.

When she's out of earshot Ava mimics her. "'Good luck, then, girls.'" Ava rolls her eyes. "Really?"

Lily asks, "What's she even doing here?"

"That little blue house." Everleigh points to a place across the street. "That's where she lives."

"Let's just play!" says Hailey. She starts splitting us into two teams. A red team and a black team, the school colours. We're wearing mismatched T-shirts, shorts and socks, but I've noticed most of the girls are wearing our school colours. Red or black. Lacy Barker is, of course, on the black team.

"Flag rugby," says Hailey. "When the defence gets your flag, stop and post the ball, place it on the ground. Each team gets five chances to score."

A few minutes into the game I realize how quick I am. Sarah tries to dodge past me but I snatch her flag.

Everleigh has good speed but I zero in on her and steal her flag from behind.

Lightning Lily tries some fancy footwork on me. I keep an eye on her midsection. It's hard to fake with your waist. She tries to fake one way, then the other. I lunge for her flag, she spins to escape and — *pow!* Her shoulder hammers me in the mouth.

I stagger back a step and plunk onto my butt. For a second I'm dazed.

"Sorry," Lily says. She offers me a hand up.

My fingers go to my bottom lip. There's a smudge of blood. "No worries." I hop up. "I'm good."

The first time I get the ball in my hands I'm running toward a solid wall of defence. Hailey has taught the girls to come up in a line, as a team. But I see a gap between Hannah and Bobbi. I dart through, and Bobbi reaches for my flag, but I skip past and race for the goal line.

The next time I get the ball I only have Tara to beat. She's crouched low, ready to shift left or right. A couple metres away from her I fake right, plant my foot and vault to the left. Tara is turned just enough for me to escape. I dash past her and sprint for the line.

After the game, doing a cool-down lap, I trot up to Sarah.

"Hey, speed merchant!" she teases. "Did I count five scores?"

"Missed one." I trot backward in front of her.

"That lip, it's gone insta-fat."

I gingerly touch a finger to my bottom lip. It's as fat as a breakfast sausage.

"You could enter that lip in the Fall Fair. And how's your knee?" Sarah somehow knows all my secrets.

I realize that once we got going I forgot all about my knee. But that's three serious bumps — shoulder, knee and lip. And we haven't even played a real game of rugby yet! That little voice in the back of my head asks the question again, *is rugby really for you, Maddy?*

Hailey calls us in under the posts. "Good run, girls. We're really starting to look like a team."

It seems to me like we really are a team. There are girls from all kinds of backgrounds — wrestling, hockey, boxing, basketball. But we're all getting along. Everybody is loving it.

"Don't look now," says Ava, "but I think someone is spying on us."

I get a glimpse of Ms. O peeking out from behind her drapes.

"She's watching," says Bobbi.

Ms. O has a phone to her ear.

"I'll bet she's ratting us out right now," says Ava.

11 SOLO

The next morning, first block of the day, I'm alone at a table in the school library. At the checkout desk, a single student whispers to the librarian. The only other sound is the hum of the old heating system.

I Google "rugby," and get sucked right in. There's a million sites about everything rugby. Old black and white videos, stuff about strategies, player positions, old championships. It goes on and on.

My inspirational essay for Ms. O is due tomorrow. I'm worried, and I should be working on it. It's well-written, but rugby doesn't seem to be Ms. O's favourite thing right now. It's too late to change the topic. And honestly I don't want to. Kayla Moleschi truly is inspirational. She's determined, totally focused and she has dedicated years of her life to the game. I love her story.

I wonder — could I ever make a difference on the field? Not a Kayla difference, just a high school difference. I'm pretty quick. Maybe I can make that work for me.

I pull up YouTube, and stuff my earbuds in. I click on a thirty-second snippet of a women's game. Canada is playing Ireland. Canada has the ball and number eleven, a winger, is racing down the sideline.

"It looks like she's in trouble," says the Irish announcer. "There's a solid wall of green jerseys in front of her."

Number eleven kicks the ball. It's a short kick, kind of like a grounder in baseball. It slices right through a gap in the green defenders and hops along the turf.

"That's a perfect wee grubber," says the announcer. "Now, will it hop up for her?"

Number eleven sprints after the ball. The Irish have spun around and they're chasing, right on her heels. The ball pops up just right for number eleven to grab.

"It sits up perfectly!" yells the commentator. "A brilliant little grubber kick."

The Canadian player dashes full speed, and dives in to score a try.

I watch it again. Then in slow motion.

I Google "grubber kick." It's a kick designed to roll and tumble irregularly along the ground, making it difficult for the defence to handle. Sometimes the ball will "sit up" with an uncanny "hop" for the offensive players to catch.

I keep searching rugby kicking techniques. Another cool way to beat the defence is a chip kick. It's a short kick that goes over top of the defenders, designed for the kicker to retrieve.

By the time the bell rings, my rugby IQ has skyrocketed. And I've got a new focus. I'm going to learn to kick!

The library door opens and a flood of students streams in. Mrs. Levens is at the back of the group. She gives me a little wave and walks over.

My pulse picks up. I nibble the inside of my cheek.

"Maddy," she says. Her voice is soft. "What happened to your lip?"

"Sometimes I lead with my face," I try to joke.

"Your teeth?"

"Just a flesh wound." I say it like I'm an old pro.

"I worry about you." She drops a stack of marking on the table. "It's such a brutal game for girls."

"And for boys?" I surprise myself. I'm challenging her.

"Either way," she says. "It's a barbaric game, Maddy. I watched a game, or at least I tried to watch, when I was in university. A guy on the ground got stepped on so badly it ripped half the shirt off his back."

"Those were the old days, when raking with your cleats was allowed." I tell her like I've known it forever. But the fact is I learned it this morning. "But it's changed. In the modern game you can't do anything like that. One touch with your boot and the ref blows it up."

"And those scrums." She shakes her head. "Like dog piles with no rules. It's a wonder someone doesn't get killed!"

"Scrums are the most controlled parts of the game. Everyone has a specific position and a certain way to bind. A scrum is like a well-oiled machine. The refs are very careful with rules about how the scrums engage." I'm almost over my head. I'm repeating what I read just a few minutes ago. "And I just found out," I say, "they're not rules. In rugby they are laws."

"Well, there should be a law against it." She plunks into a chair.

"I'll survive, Mrs. Levens." I throw my bag over my shoulder. "And don't you worry, I'll be ready to play." She knows I'm talking about volleyball.

The hallway is elbow to elbow with kids on the way to class. I get a glimpse of Ben coming my way.

"Maddy!" He stops in front of me and looks right at my lip. "That's a beauty! Let me get a look." He comes in so close I get a whiff of his spearmint gum. "You're getting pretty tough, Nutty." He says it like a compliment.

"Really sucks, what happened at the practice," I say.

"Yeah. Sharma had a big yell-fest at me and Fiss in the office." Ben looks down and toes the floor with one foot. "But coaching?" he say. "I think it would be really tough."

I wonder if he's trying to cover up how disappointed he is. Did he really want to coach us?

"I think you'd be great," I say. "You'd be a cool coach."

"I don't know, Nutty."

"Do you have a rugby ball?" I change the subject. "That I could use for a bit?"

"Sure," he shrugs. "How come?"

"I want to kick," I say. "And I need to practice."

"You want to be a kicker?"

"Sort of."

"Come on." He starts walking. "I've got one in my locker." He stops and puts his finger to his forehead, like he just got an idea. "The team has practice balls," he says. "We've got a whole bag. I could it sign out."

"Okay?" I say it like a question.

"I'll get them for you." He turns into his classroom. "After school."

★★★

At the end of the day I lug the net bag of eight practice balls to the middle school. It's a couple blocks from my place. There's a little field behind the school where no one will see me. I look around. No one is watching.

I try to kick a grubber kick. It's terrible. The ball goes off the side of my foot and totally off target. The next kick isn't much better. I pull out my phone and go to a tutorial.

"Hold the ball north–south," the guy with an English accent says. "Knee over the foot, strike the top half of the ball."

My next kick is better. It actually heads toward my target. I'm thinking that those years of minor soccer might pay off. After a few kicks I try it at a jog. It's not as easy, but I focus and make sure of the basics.

The sun slowly sinks toward the hills. After kicking about a million grubbers I'm totally pooped. I can kick standing still. Running and kicking is super tough. But every once in a while the ball hops into my hands like in the videos. It's just enough to give me hope. By the time I head for home, my T-shirt is sweat-stuck all across my back.

12 A Coach WITH CRED

Mom's monthly trip to the city Costco is always a big hit with the girls. I hop in the passenger seat of our SUV. Sarah, Everleigh and Hailey slide in the back. We've got a plan. Mom is going to drop us at the rugby field while she grabs a couple things. Hailey's old team is playing in a big game.

"It should be a great match," says Hailey. "There will be two totally different styles. My old team, South Road, is all about speed and getting the ball out to their backs. Wildfire is the opposite. Their big forwards want to keep the ball tight."

"So there is a strategy to rugby," Mom observes. She eases the SUV through our neighbourhood. "Not just a bunch of girls trying to crunch each other."

"Now you sound like Dad," I say. He got all pouty and quiet when he saw my lip. That was a few days ago. Today it's almost back to normal. And so is Dad.

"Oh, yeah," says Hailey. "Rugby is the most complicated game out there. Like a game of chess.

Both teams are looking for the other guy's weakness."

"I'll have to pay closer attention." Mom turns the car onto Main Street and says, "there's your favourite English teacher."

Ms. O is walking her old dog on the other side of the street.

"Favourite?" says Everleigh. "Not mine."

"Favourite grammar cop," says Sarah.

"Did you tell the girls?" asks Mom.

Everleigh leans forward to get a look at me. "Tell us what?"

"Got an A on my Kayla Moleschi essay." I hate bragging.

"No way!" says Hailey. "Suck up."

"Ms. O hasn't given out an A since . . ." Sarah rubs her chin, pretends to be serious. "Since 1999."

"And it's weird." I turn backward to face the girls. "When she gave me back my essay she asked a strange question. She asked if I knew when the first game of women's rugby was played around here."

"That *is* weird. So when?" says Sarah.

"March 6, 1977," I say. "Douglas College played UBC. Ms. O told me."

"How were you supposed to know that?" says Everleigh.

"What I wonder is," Sarah asks, "how does Ms. O know that?

A Coach with Cred

An hour later Mom pulls into the gravel parking lot at the City rugby grounds. "Back in an hour or so," she tells us.

The teams are still warming up and there's a good-sized crowd. The sun is warm overhead, and a gentle breeze catches the corner flags. Smoke curls above the concession. The sticky barbeque aroma it carries makes my stomach growl.

"I smell bacon," Everleigh sniffs the air.

"They do wicked bacon cheddar cheeseburgers." Hailey points to the concession.

"I'm starving," I say.

"Lunch time, girls." Sarah starts marching straight for the concession lineup.

It takes a while for the bacon cheeseburgers, but it's well worth the wait. My burger is massive. When I take my first bite, the hefty patty tries to escape out the back of the bun.

We stand shoulder to shoulder with the sideline rope tight at our waists. The game is a few minutes in. A glob of barbeque sauce oozes down my wrist. I lick it off.

South Road is in green kit, defending at their twenty-two metre line. The first thing I notice about Wildfire is that they are all big beefy players. They wear flaming red jerseys.

"Are they seniors?" Everleigh asks with a cheek full of burger.

"Nope." Hailey uses a napkin to wipe her mouth. "Juniors. But they're big, eh?"

I wonder, *are we going to play against players that big?*

A Wildfire forward charges straight upfield. A green player wraps her up, but the runner keeps pumping her legs. A couple of her teammates latch on and drive her forward.

She finally gets dragged to the ground. A swarm of red players drive over her and the ball. A Wildfire girl snatches the ball from the back of the ruck and powers forward.

"They'll do that all day," says Hailey. "It's called pick and drive. Keep the ball tight in the pack. Short run, ruck over and the next player picks up and goes. *Bam!* Right into the heavy traffic."

There's a Wildfire knock-on and the ref chirps his whistle. "Set scrum, green."

"South Road has a totally different strategy," Hailey explains. "They want to get the ball wide. Away from the big Wildfire forwards and out to their speedy backs."

South Road wins the scrum. But before their scrum half can get a pass away, she takes a thumping tackle. The ball pops loose. A Wildfire flanker gets her hands on it and bashes into the nearest green defender.

"Those Wildfire players love contact," says Sarah.

"That's their game." Hailey pops the last of her burger in her mouth. "They run north, south, straight up the field. A big girl's game."

Exactly the style I have to avoid, I think. It would turn me into peanut butter.

"Go, go, go!" Everleigh shouts.

The Wildfire number three is a big thundering prop. She stiff-arms a tackler and breaks into space. With charging high knees, she plows over the green fullback and plunks over the try line.

"Now that's rugby!" says Hailey.

"She's a powerhouse," Everleigh says. "Steamrolls anybody in her way."

That's what scares me.

Sarah has me in the corner of her eye. She's looking for my reaction.

"Great run." I put on a weak smile but a pool of fear has settled in my gut.

In the second half Wildfire scores two more tries.

"There's your mom," says Everleigh. Mom is walking toward us. "Can we stay, Mrs. B?" Everleigh pleads.

"Only a few minutes left," says Hailey.

"Sure, I'll get a coffee." Mom wanders toward the concession. A couple minutes later she's laughing with a very tall woman.

"I know that woman from somewhere," Hailey says, watching the two of them chat.

"Whoa, she's pretty," Everleigh says and stares. "Like that supermodel. Tyra Banks kind of pretty."

I think I recognize the woman too. She doesn't look like a supermodel to me, but she is really pretty. She looks like the woman I saw on YouTube talking about lineout strategies. I'm not sure.

In the last minutes of the game, South Road can't defend the endless Wildfire attack. When the ref blows the final whistle, the score is twenty-seven–nil.

Thinking about playing a team as big and ferocious as Wildfire has me rattled.

When we get back to the SUV I climb in the back. Everleigh has shotgun. Sometimes she talks to my mom like Mom is one of the girls. "You're such a social butterfly, Mrs. B," she says. "Two minutes at the field and you're making new friends."

"Maybe I take after you, Everleigh," Mom jokes. "It's contagious."

"The lady you were talking to," Hailey asks, "who is she?"

"She's new in town, an outreach nurse. I met her at work. But here's the thing — she has a rugby background, and she might want to coach."

"Us?" asks Everleigh. "Coach us?"

Mom reaches back and hands me a business card. "She said you should call her."

"Is she certified?" Hailey asks.

"You'll have to ask her."

"Call her!" Everleigh twists around and gives my knee a slap. "Call her, Maddy!"

"No time like the present, Peanut." Sarah slaps my other knee.

"Might as well," Hailey says and tries to hand me her phone.

I push it away. "Just give me a sec. What am I supposed to say?" I dig my phone out of my pocket.

"Just tell her we really, really, need a coach." Everleigh stuffs a knuckle between her teeth.

"We're super keen," says Hailey.

Sarah grabs my wrist. "But tell her we're rookies. Okay?"

"Just tell her . . ." Mom pauses. "Just be yourself, Maddy."

"Okay, okay." I bite my inner cheek. "Give me a sec." I take a long, ragged breath and punch the numbers.

A warm voice answers. "Hello?"

"Yes, hello." I sound so not myself. Formal. And my voice is up an octave. Everleigh reaches over and hits the speaker button on my phone. "This is Maddy Borkowski speaking?" I say like it's a question. "You know my mother?"

"Oh, yeah," she says. "You guys are starting a rugby team. Cool. I'd like to swing by for a look."

A look? What does that mean?

"Tell her where we practice," Hailey whispers.

"We practice Mondays and Wednesdays after school at Rotary Park," I say.

"Sounds good. I can't make it this week but I'll see you a week from Monday. My email, if you want, is katekolisi at Gmail. See you then."

I hang up.

"Kate Kolisi! I knew I recognized her!" Hailey punches the roof. "*The* Kate Kolisi! She's a legend!"

"How come?" asks Everleigh.

Hailey is wide-eyed and smiling like she just won the lotto. "Kate Kolisi played rugby for Canada."

13 Bring IT ON

At Monday's practice I can feel the pressure. A tremor of excitement dances around in my stomach.

"We want to look good for next week," says Hailey. By now everyone knows Kate Kolisi played for Canada. "She's going to watch us practice next week and see if we're the real thing. We have one shot."

It's a perfect afternoon. The sky is blue. There's a whisper of a breeze and not a cloud in the sky. Hailey has explained the basics of a new drill.

"It should have some flow once we get it going." Hailey has the ball in hand and she runs at Bobbi, who's holding a crash pad. Hailey pauses right before contact. "Load up your legs like steel springs." She dips into a powerful crouch. "Then, *pow!*" Hailey explodes into the pad shoulder-first. The pad jerks back, Hailey goes to ground and posts the ball, placing it on the ground. Bobbi steps over her and braces the pad again.

Tara has been briefed. She comes in low and hard. She drives Bobbi and her pad backward.

Hailey keeps instructing from the ground. "Everleigh, you're scrum-half. You take the ball."

Everleigh snaps up the ball and throws a long pass to me. I pass out to our backs and the ball goes hand to hand down the line.

"Great job, guys!" Hailey throws a punch into the air. "We've got it."

Sarah jogs over and leans her shoulder against mine. "Don't look now," she says. "But our biggest fan has her front row seat."

Ms. O is in her front yard with a pair of garden shears. She snips at the hedge, but she's watching us.

Ava sees what we're looking at. "I'll bet she's got a job. Watchdog for the City. We could be screwed."

"Here comes trouble," Hannah says, pointing down the street.

Down the street is a squad of guys. They're coming our way.

"Boys' team," I say. They must have just finished their practice. They're still wearing their gear. Ben is with half a dozen others. When they get to the park they stop to watch.

"Lookin' good, girls," calls Jack Davis. I can't tell if he's being sarcastic. He's a lanky scrummer with enough confidence to grow a scraggy mullet.

My palms start getting sweaty. The guys have never watched us practice.

Dion Lomavatu hangs his muscled arms over the fence. He's got cinnamon skin and an afro. Popular guy. If anyone is going to throw the girls off their game, it's Dion.

"Can we get in on the action?" stocky Bo Basra calls out. I know Bo pretty well. I can tell he's just being a nice guy.

"What about a challenge?" Ben asks. "The seven of us will take on your whole crew."

"Touch?" Dion suggests. "What about a game of two-hand touch?"

"I'll play touch." Ava stops in her tracks.

"Okay." Hailey holds up her hands to stop the banter. "You guys want to put your money where your mouth is? Tackle. Bring it on!"

Hailey lays out the rules. It's a small grid so we'll play seven against five.

We lose the toss and kick off to the boys. Jack leaps up and snatches the ball out of the air. He bounds forward. Just as Lily is about to make the first tackle, he fires a long spin pass wide to Dion.

Dion fakes like he's going wide, cuts inside and does a spin move that leaves Ava flat-footed.

The guys score twice more before Tara sneaks through a gap to make it three to one. In the next play, Hailey dives to catch Bo. She tears a strip off the bottom of his T-shirt. Both teams slow down for a laugh. Even Lacy Barker has a giggle.

I sub off and amble over to Ben on the sideline.

"You guys rock," he says.

"Be careful," I say. "You haven't seen our secret weapon."

He lifts one foot and claws a lump of sod from his cleats. "What's your secret weapon?"

"You'll see."

On the field Bobbi drops her shoulder and knocks Bo on his butt. It gets everyone laughing again.

"She's a powerhouse." Ben stuffs his knuckles in his mouth like he's petrified. He trots onto the field and gives Bo a high-five. Bo is faking a big limp to get an extra laugh.

A couple minutes later, Hailey calls, "Water break." She brings all the girls in for a tight huddle. "Make the ball do the work," she explains. "Just pass to where the defence is thin. We've got an overlap every time."

The boys kick off to us. I make the catch. But when I look up, both Bo and Dion are coming at me fast. I run at them a couple steps, holding the ball in both hands. Then I drop it on my foot and boot a little grubber kick. It shoots right between the two defenders. Perfect!

I sprint after it and the boys turn to chase me. My kick had a little bit too much weight. The ball is headed for the sideline and I'm not going to be able to catch up. I race, but the ball skitters out of bounds.

"I didn't know we're allowed to kick!" Bo pants.

"You can kick a grubber?" Dion throws me a high-five.

Ben appears right in front of me. "Amazing," he says. "A grubber!"

The boys score the next couple tries. Hailey blows a whistle to end the game and I look across the street. Ms. O still has the garden shears but she's sitting on her stairs. Just watching.

"Surprised us," says Jack. "You guys are stellar!"

The guys have nothing but good things to say about our play.

"I'm gonna put five bucks in your GoFundMe," says Bo.

"Big spender." Dion gives him a playful shove.

"How's it going?" Ben asks me. "The GoFundMe?" He sits at my feet and starts pulling his cleats off.

"Pretty slow," I say.

"I'll get my old man to throw a few bucks in," he says.

14 Big MONEY

The next day, Sarah and I are at our locker. Everleigh and Hailey come around the corner.

"The guys are having a bake sale," says Everleigh.

"And there's cinnamon buns," Hailey adds.

"With icing?" Sarah asks.

"And look at this." Everleigh holds up a key. "For the old equipment room."

"We going to rob the place?" Sarah jokes.

"Cinnamon buns first," says Hailey.

We stuff our books in our lockers and head for the bake sale. Ben and Jack are behind the table. Both of them are sporting their moms' aprons.

"Special deal for rugby players," says Jack. "Anything on the table, one dollar."

"Nice aprons," says Sarah.

"Martha Stewart." Jack does a twirl.

At first business is slow, and only a few students come to the table. Minutes later a crowd arrives. Jack can't talk and serve at the same time. Ben isn't any better. So Sarah, Hailey, Everleigh and I all step behind the table to help. Most of the items sell in about ten minutes.

"Heads up." Sarah gives me an elbow. "Levens alert."

Mrs. Levens strides up to the table and gives us a thin smile. "For the rugby team?"

"Everything is a dollar." I don't tell her which rugby team.

Mrs. Levens points at the last of the cookies and a few sad-looking squares. "For the staff room," she says. "I heard you're getting a coach."

"Kate Kolisi." I put her goods in a little cardboard box.

"Does she know anything about coaching?" Mrs. Levens slides a five-dollar bill across the table.

"She played for Canada." I hold out a hand, palm up. Doesn't that say it all?

"Just because someone is a great player doesn't mean they can coach," she says. "I've taken a dozen coaching courses and it's a lot more than bump, set, spike. Coaching psychology. It's a science."

She lets that sink in. I look for support, but the boys are counting money and Sarah and Everleigh pretend to wipe crumbs. Hailey is suddenly glued to her phone.

"And what about first aid? I have a level two, just for volleyball." Mrs. Levens drops her voice to a dramatic whisper. "And there's no scrums or body slamming.

What if one of those dog piles collapses, someone gets a serious injury and —"

"She's a registered nurse," Hailey pipes up.

"Oh?" I can tell Mrs. Levens is surprised. She tightens her lips into a thin line and picks up her box of goodies. "I guess that's one step in the right direction." She turns and strides down the hall.

"When does your coach show up?" Jack asks.

"Monday," says Everleigh.

"Uniforms?" Ben asks. "When will you get your gear?"

"Not yet," says Sarah. "But there might be some used stuff in the old equipment room."

"But you need gear." Jack gives Ben an obvious elbow.

"Oh, yeah." Ben picks up the plastic box full of cash. He turns to face me. "This is for you," he stammers. "For the girls, I mean. The girls' team." He hands me the box.

It's heavy with coins and a few bills. And a chunk of paper sticking out the top says, "IOU $6."

"I ate all the brownies." Jack nods at the IOU. "But if we're going to be a real rugby school, we need a girls' team too."

"I did the math." Ben rolls his eyes. "There's almost enough in there to buy half a dozen pairs of socks."

"Thanks anyway, guys," says Everleigh.

"Yeah, thanks," Hailey and I echo.

"We know where there might be a stash." Everleigh holds up the key between thumb and forefinger. "The old equipment room."

"Really?" says Jack.

"Good luck." There's a twinge of sarcasm in Ben's voice.

"We'll see." Everleigh turns and heads down the hall. Hailey, Sarah and I follow to the equipment room. It's jam-packed with tall stacks of boxes and bins. There are old computers piled chest high and the place has the musty smell of ancient textbooks.

"Where do we start?" asks Hailey.

"We're looking for a box marked 2010," says Everleigh. "But we can take any uniforms we find."

Hailey wrestles a 2010 bin from a wall of teetering boxes. Inside there are nine old jerseys.

"Pink?" Hailey holds one at arm's length.

"Guess they used to be red," I murmur.

"I'm not wearing pink." Hailey shakes her head.

"Look at this." Everleigh is digging in another bin. "The old cheerleading stuff."

"Lord help us." Sarah pinches the bridge of her nose. "Please tell me we are not going into battle dressed in pleated skirts and pink tops."

"I could sew this stuff." Everleigh holds up a black cheerleader skirt that looks like it dates back a hundred years. "I sew a lot. This could be a perfect pair of rugby shorts."

Hailey and Sarah both look at me.

"Nothing to lose," I shrug.

★★★

A couple hours later we're in Everleigh's dining room. There's a long elegant table with high-back chairs. Everleigh has the cheerleading stuff spread across the table. Sarah, Hailey and I have been given instructions on exact shapes to cut out of the old skirt fabric.

Everleigh is hunched over the sewing machine. "Almost done." The machine whirs. "First one will fit Hailey." Everleigh turns away from the machine and holds up a pair of shorts. In her other hand is one of the pink shirts.

"The shorts look lovely," Sarah says, hiding a smirk. "The top?" She presses a finger to her lips, pretending she's deep in thought. "I'm thinking we could be cartoon characters. Miss Piggy?"

"Just try them on." Everleigh throws them at Hailey.

Hailey disappears into the living room. A minute later she hobbles out. The shorts are knee length and so tight she can barely walk.

I start to laugh.

"Is that a penguin impression, Hailey?" Sarah asks.

Hailey tugs at the puffy shoulder of her top.

Sarah strikes a model's pose. "Ple-ease," she makes

the word sound like two syllables. "I wanna be an eighties disco diva."

Even Everleigh has to laugh.

"We've still got these." I pull out a pair of pompoms.

Everleigh is right back on her phone. Probably looking for a better sewing pattern.

"How about this?" Sarah has pulled on a cheerleading shirt and one of the pink tops. "We could be in *Sports Illustrated*."

Hailey throws a shirt at her, then a pompom at me. I lurch back and stumble over a chair.

"Holy crap!" Everleigh is still looking at her phone. Then she says it again, in a whisper. "Holy crap."

"What?" I clamber to my feet.

Everleigh stares at us, wide-eyed.

"What is it?" I ask again.

Everleigh turns the screen to face us. She's speechless.

I step close to read what's there. "Holy crap . . ." My hand goes to my mouth.

"I ain't looking." Sarah looks terrified. "It's contagious, I ain't looking."

"Let me see," Hailey says and takes the phone. "Wow . . ." Hailey falls into a chair.

Finally Sarah looks at the phone.

The GoFundMe has received a donation. A huge one.

"That's amazing," says Hailey. "Who was it?"

Everleigh scrolls. "Doesn't say."

I think back. At the park Ben had said, "I'll get my old man to throw in a few bucks." I wonder if it was Mr. Horvat.

"One thing's for sure," I throw a pink uniform into the corner. "We won't be wearing these."

15 PROOF

It's Sunday afternoon and my favourite aroma fills the house. Roast turkey. The Horvats will be here for dinner in a couple of hours.

I trot down the stairs with my rugby cleats hanging over my shoulder. I'm dragging the bag of practice balls. They *thump-bump* down each stair.

"Kicking practice?" Dad asks.

"At the middle school," I say. "Back in about an hour."

Dad pecks a kiss on top of my head as I go by. He's been pretty good about the rugby lately.

"Did you donate to our GoFundMe?" I ask.

"Oh, crap." He pats his back pocket where he keeps his wallet. "Not yet. I was going to —"

"Sorry, that's not what I mean. Someone made a really big anonymous donation," I explain. "Was it you, Dad?"

I can tell by the surprised look on his face it wasn't him.

"I haven't yet," he says. "But I will, for sure."

The field is deserted. The sun is warm on my face. I drop the bag of balls in front of the soccer goal. If I can kick one good kick in each game, it might make up for my size.

Chip kicking is my focus for today. I want to kick over the cross bar, just right, so I can run forward and catch it.

I jog slowly toward the goal and chip a little kick over the cross bar. I sprint after it, my eye on the ball. The kick is a bit long. I race, stretch out my arms, but the ball comes down just beyond my reach.

The next chip kick is better. It's a little higher over the cross bar. I chase hard, get under the ball and I make the catch in cradled arms.

Out of my first ten kicks I catch two. After forty kicks I've lost count of how many I've caught. But I'm feeling good. I'm breathing hard and dripping sweat. It's time to head home.

By dinnertime I'm showered, my hair in a ponytail, right in time for the Horvats. Dad sits at the end of the table. He loves tradition and makes a big production of sharpening the carving knife. The twins love the performance. After the knife is perfectly sharpened, he starts carving the turkey.

Ben is sitting across from me like always. He arrived late on his bike. Just in time to wash up and sit at the table.

"If I remember," Dad says, busy slicing, "a drumstick for Emma, and white meat only for Anna."

The twins beam and hold out their plates for Dad to fill.

"And Peanut." He scratches his head like he's trying to remember. "A slice of white and a slice of dark."

"Perfect." I send my plate down the table.

"I hear you girls are playing some good rugby," says Mr. Horvat.

"You bet. We're finally starting to get lots of girls out. And our GoFundMe just got a huge donation." I watch Mr. Horvat's face for his reaction.

"No kidding?" He drains his water glass. "I'll have to put in a couple bucks myself."

"How much is in there?" asks Ben.

"Enough for brand new gear. Jerseys, shorts, socks, already ordered." I keep an eye on Mr. Horvat, but he's focused on opening a bottle of wine. He looks totally innocent. I guess it's still a mystery.

"Good for you," says Mrs. Horvat. "I hear you're pretty fast out there, Maddy."

"Takes after her mom," says Dad. He surprises me, talking positively about rugby. "Pin Ball Penny."

"Oh, stop." Mom gives him a playful swat.

Mom serves two types of pie for dessert. Cherry and apple. She says to Mrs. Horvat, "I made you a pie to take home. Don't let me forget."

"I'll take it out," I offer. The parents' conversation is droning on about local politics. It's a good excuse to escape. I'm on my feet before anyone else can volunteer.

I place the boxed pie safely on the back seat of the Horvats' car. I shut the car door and turn to head back inside.

"Think fast!" Ben tosses a Frisbee in my direction from the front steps of the house. I make the catch and zing it back to him. Ben has to hustle down the stairs and into the garden to save my throw from hitting the window. He throws it back. It's a perfect pass, right into my hands. Dad has got a little sprinkler going on the side garden. I think of throwing the Frisbee so Ben has to get wet.

"When are you getting uniforms?" he asks.

Before I can answer, Dad comes out the door. "I need to turn that sprinkler off," he says. "It's nearly drowning the petunias."

"Think fast!" Ben tosses a soft pass to Dad. Dad lurches a step and snags the Frisbee.

"You think Maddy is going to be a rugby star?" Ben asks.

"We haven't decided yet." Dad tosses to me. He means he hasn't decided if he wants me to play or not. He asks me, "You like all that tackling, Maddy?"

"I love it!" I whip the Frisbee to Ben and he leaps to catch it. "Tell you what, Dad." I put my hands on my hips. "If I could tackle you, would that prove it? That rugby is the game for me?"

"Fat chance," he says. "I played linebacker in high school." He does a bodybuilder pose.

Ben throws Dad a long pass that hangs up in the air. The Frisbee floats high across the yard. Dad trots along, keeping his eye on it.

This is my chance. I take off and run up behind Dad. Just as he makes the catch, I shout, "Think fast!" He spots me just as I'm diving in for a shoestring tackle. I get my arms around both ankles and lock my hands together.

Dad thumps to the ground, laughing. "Holy crap," he snorts. "You tackled your old man!"

"I guess that settles it," says Ben. "Proof. If Nutty can tackle you, Mr. B, she can tackle anybody."

16 ALL IN

The next day at Rotary Park we're doing a warm-up stretch under a damp overcast sky. I've got a gut full of butterflies. This is the day Kate Kolisi is going to watch us practice.

The uniforms haven't arrived, but the word has spread to all the girls on the team. Wear your team colours. We bend to stretch in mismatched gear, various shades of red and black.

Parm and Preet Singh are out for the first time. They are willowy girls with waist-length black hair.

"We've got fifteen!" Everleigh grabs my bicep. "Finally! Enough for a team."

That's so cool, I think.

Word about Kate Kolisi has been flying around the school. Leah Chan is out for the first time too. She's a thickset pale girl. Maybe the smartest kid in school. I don't think she's ever played a sport.

"Hi," I say. "Great to see you out." I put out my fist.

She gives it a little bump and in a tiny voice she says, "Hi."

Hailey calls us into a tight circle. "Listen up." I can tell she's stoked. Wide-eyed. She throws her arms around the girls on either side of her. "We need to look good today. This is our one chance."

A green SUV with a Public Health graphic on the doors pulls up to the gate.

"That's her!" Only Everleigh can whisper loud enough for everyone to hear.

Kate is taller than I remember. Maybe it's her towering messy bun that makes her look so big. She walks through the gate with a ball palmed in one hand.

We stare. There's a moment of silence. All the girls are frozen. It's like a beam of light should break through the clouds. Light her up like in a cheesy movie.

Hailey pulls it together and steps forward. "Hi, Kate," she says, holding out her hand.

"Great to meet you!" Kate shakes Hailey's hand and pulls her in for a quick hug. She moves through our group, one to the next, and shakes our hands.

"Nice to meet you, Maddy." She squeezes my hand. It's a warm, dry vice grip.

"I love your tattoo." Everleigh points to the big maple leaf on Kate's thigh with the number thirty-four above it.

"I'm very proud of it," says Kate.

"Why thirty-four?" asks Everleigh.

Kate pulls up the hem of her faded rugby shorts so we get a better look. The maple leaf is bright red on her dark skin. Her quads are beefy and bulging muscle.

"Thirty-four," says Kate. "The number of times I played for Canada."

"Who did you play against?" asks Ava.

"What position?" Hailey asks.

Kate gets hit with questions from every direction.

"What was it like?"

"Do you sign autographs?

"Give the poor woman a chance." I hold up my hands for everyone to shut up.

Kate smiles. She tells us she moved to Canada from Uganda when she was six, started playing rugby at thirteen and never looked back. "For Canada, I played second row and number eight against England, New Zealand, France and the USA. The strongest countries in the world. And you know what?" she says. "Any of you can do it. I was just a skinny teenager with a big heart. All it takes is commitment and hard work."

For a second I let myself daydream. I look down at my leg and imagine my own tattoo.

"Enough about me," says Kate. "How about you guys? Show me what you've been doing."

Hailey takes the lead and gets us to demonstrate a couple passing drills. Bobbi drops an easy pass, so does Lily. Tara trips over her own feet and I throw a pass at Sarah's legs. Nerves are getting the best of us.

Hailey switches us to our tackle drill. Kate watches a couple tackles then stops us.

"You guys have nailed the basics. And I'm seeing a lot of natural athletes," she says. "Show me one more hit. Hailey, can you be the tackler?" Kate throws Sarah a ball. "And can you be the runner, Sarah?"

"Oh, I get it," Sarah says as she trots toward the sideline to wait for Hailey's tackle. "I'm the crash test dummy."

Hailey is our best tackler. She goes in low and hard and makes a textbook tackle. I'm glad it's not me carrying the ball.

"Beauty," says Kate. "Nice job. I love that you placed the ball, Sarah, after you were tackled. Everyone knows you have to release the ball when you're tackled?"

All of us nod.

"That very short time after the tackle is called the breakdown," Kate explains. "Games are won or lost at the breakdown. This time, Hailey, I want you to make the tackle, pop up on your feet, and grab the ball."

Hailey goes in low again and makes a good tackle. Then she scrambles to her feet and snatches the ball.

"Beauty!" says Kate. "Now everyone find a partner and give it a go."

I'm with Tara. She drives me into the turf. When it's my turn to tackle, I hit her low, then bounce to my feet and scoop up the ball.

"Perfect!" says Kate. "You're super quick, Maddy. Let's add another player to the drill. Hailey, you tackle Sarah again. If I'm Sarah's first teammate arriving at the tackle, I want to either grab the ball myself, or drive Hailey off of it. Let's try in slow motion."

We watch Hailey tackle Sarah. When Hailey pops up to her feet and is trying to pick up the ball, Kate shows us what she'd do if she was Sarah's teammate. "I'd try to get under Hailey. Shoulder to shoulder." Kate gently drives Hailey off the ball.

"If Hailey is solid over the ball," says Kate, "maybe I can't move her. So I use an alligator roll." Kate wraps her arms around Hailey's torso and rolls her to one side away from the ball.

"It's like wrestling," says Hannah.

"Exactly," says Kate. She stays lying on the ground and explains, "I'm always hoping that the first person to the breakdown is one of my players, to get possession of the ball."

We're listening intently, standing shoulder to shoulder.

"I like the way you break everything into little pieces," says Hailey.

"There's a lot to think about," says Everleigh. "Am I smart enough for this?"

"You are," says Kate. "But you're right. Every time you arrive at a breakdown, there's a decision to make. Should I go for the ball? Or should I drive the opposition off?"

"Oh, crap," says Ava. She points at the gate.

Ms. O has crossed the street and she's storming straight toward us. I've never seen her move so fast. Her cane is barely touching the ground.

Everyone watches. Kate turns to see what we're looking at. Ms. O comes hoofing through the gate. She stops in front of Kate. "Could we have a word?"

Ms. O turns and shuffles back toward the gate. Kate follows. I can't hear, but I see Ms. O pointing her cane at one area of the field, then another. Kate nods. Ms. O turns, then stumps out through the gate and across the street.

"Not a big deal," Kate tells us. "She's worried. Says we should move to another area of the field, not tear up the grass."

Kate moves us to another section of the field. As practice comes to a close, she leads us in a slow cool-down trot.

Hailey jogs next to me. "How did we do?" I whisper.

"Don't know." Hailey's face is pinched. She looks worried.

We've finally got enough players, I think. *If Kate will coach, I'm sure we'll find a teacher sponsor.*

Kate stops us and we circle up to stretch.

"Are you going to coach us?" Everleigh blurts.

Kate keeps doing a side bend stretch. We all do the same. Then Kate looks down and touches her hands to her toes.

My heart sinks. I thought we did pretty well.

"There's nothing I'd rather do." Kate beams a smile. "I'm all in!"

17 In the LEAGUE

When I get home my Maddy List is on the kitchen counter. It's a few little jobs Mom leaves for me to do after school. I peel and chop garlic. The sticky bits glue to my fingers.

There's a pound of ground beef in the fridge and I'm guessing dinner will be Dad's world famous tacos. I hear his pickup pull in, crunching gravel in the driveway.

"Hey, Peanut." Dad slides his hefty metal lunch kit onto the counter.

I open my arms for a hug. He gets me in our usual headlock and smacks a kiss on top of my head. Dad is straight out of the bush. I get a whiff of pine trees, sweat and diesel. There's a twig still clinging to his shoulder.

He sits at one of the island stools. My Dad-radar says something is going on. He's got his worried look. Mom calls it his puppy-dog eyes. "Sit down a sec, Peanut." He pulls a stool out for me.

It looks like this might be a rare heart-to-heart.

"Here's the thing." He rolls his wedding ring between thumb and forefinger.

My heart freezes a beat.

"With the rugby . . ." There's a second of silence. He opens his big lunch kit and pulls out a sports store bag.

"A present?" I'm thinking it just might be the cool New Zealand Black Ferns jersey I saw. I reach in the bag. "A scrum cap." I know I sound disappointed.

"I read about them." Dad takes it from me and thumps his hairy knuckles on the padding. "Chock full of soft bits. Full of noggin protection."

"That's cool?" It sounds like a question. I've seen scrum caps on YouTube but none of the other girls wear one.

"I want you to wear it, Peanut." His eyes are soft. "Looks like you guys might actually get this team up and running. You wear this, you've got my blessing."

Dad never says stuff like "blessing." I know he's struggling.

"I'll start wearing it Wednesday." I give him a two-hand shove in the chest. It's like pushing on a tree trunk, but I want to lighten things up.

"Deal." He wrestles me into a headlock.

My phone chirps. I escape the headlock and look at my text.

It's Hailey: *"good news aunt will be sponsor. jerseys here wed"*

"Your timing is perfect, Dad." I show him the text. "A teacher sponsor, jerseys. That's everything."

"I guess that's it," he says. "You're up and running."

★★★

The sun is bright for Wednesday's practice. Word about girls' rugby and Kate Kolisi has flown through the school like a wildfire. I've heard people talking in the hall.

"They've got a Canada coach!"

"Brand new uniforms."

Everleigh counts the players on the field like she always does. "We've got nineteen! And that's without Hailey."

Hailey is running late, picking up our uniforms.

"Bring it in, girls," Kate calls.

My scrum cap is hidden, tucked in my shorts under a bulky sweatshirt. I pull it out and put it on. I get a couple sideways glances but everyone is focused on Kate.

"Great turnout." Kate holds her arms open wide. She catches a glimpse of my scrum cap. "Good lookin' scrum cap, Maddy. Chuck it to me a sec." She lets out a low whistle. "This is a beaut. Have a look, girls. This baby will mold to fit your head. Hollowed ear holes so you can hear."

"Can I see?" Everleigh asks.

Kate tosses it to her. "A scrum cap will minimize soft tissue injuries. Cuts, bumps, bruises. Good on you, Maddy." She beams me a smile. "This is great, enough players to try out scrum positions and a full backline. Beauty!"

Kate's positive energy is contagious. Even Lacy Barker is smiling.

In the next half hour we work on scrums and line-outs. Kate explains a basic backline. "The ball is typically passed from scrum-half to fly-half. Then inside centre, the outside centre and then to the wing. Fullback, that's where we'll try you, Maddy. For now, you come in outside the wing."

We run what Kate calls a set piece. The ball goes into the scrum and comes out the back. Everleigh picks up at the base of the scrum. Our passes move through the backs, all the way to me outside the winger.

"Beauty!" Kate throws a punch in the air. She's stoked. It's like we won a game!

"There's our biggest fan," says Ava.

I know where to look. Ms. O is at the end of her driveway with a broom.

"I saw her taking pictures," says Tara.

"Probably evidence," Ava replies. "We're chewing up the precious grass."

"We're going to add some defence," says Kate. "Just touch, not tackling." She drops a hand on my shoulder. "Maddy, from fullback, think about picking your own gap to run in with the backs. You'll do great. I like your spunk."

Kate seems to give everyone a boost. She makes me feel confident.

The next play is a set scrum, our ball. I set up directly behind the scrum, ten metres back. I'm eyeing up the spot between the centres. That's where I'll bust into the line. Kate is helping the defence. She's at fullback.

Everleigh feeds the ball into the scrum. When she picks up at the back, the defence is right on her, no time to pass. She fakes one way, then the other, trying to escape.

I see an opening on the blindside. All the defence is out wide and there's no one defending the blindside.

"Blind!" I sprint toward the blindside. "Blindside, Ev!" She fires me a desperate pass. I catch it at my shins.

Kate sees my move and she hustles to cut me off. There's no way I'll get past her. I hold the ball in both hands and chip kick over her.

It's just like I've practiced a million times. I race after my kick and keep my eye on the ball. I stretch out my arms as the ball comes down but it's just out of reach.

"Where did you learn that!" Kate wraps me in a quick clinch. "That's a beaut! You nearly caught it!"

"The uniforms!" Everleigh shouts.

Hailey is at the gate, getting out of her aunt's van. She has a huge duffle bag over her shoulder.

Kate calls for a water break and we flock over to see the uniforms. The jerseys are super-light with a cool pattern. Our wild mustang logo is rearing on the left chest. Everybody loves them. The shorts and socks are a perfect match.

"This is the best gear ever!" says Everleigh.

Each jersey, pair of shorts and pair of socks is in its own plastic bag.

"Each position has a specific number," Kate explains as she starts handing them out. "Number one goes to Bobbi Mason, at loosehead prop."

The girls all clap, like Bobbi has won some kind of prize. Bobbi holds up her jersey like it's a treasured award.

Ava and Lacy are numbers four and five. "Second row," says Kate. "The engine room of the scrum." Ava and Lacy stand side by side and I've never seen two more opposite girls. Ava with a crop top and fake eyelashes. Lacy has her black nail polish and matching eyeliner. But that's our rugby team. It has brought girls together who usually wouldn't even talk to each other. Now we bind tight together. We're sisters in arms!

"Number eight goes to our captain." Kate hands Hailey her jersey and there's more clapping, cheers and whistling. "You can lead the team from the back of the scrum," says Kate.

Everleigh gets number nine. "Scrum-half," Kate tells us. "We need someone who can direct traffic and isn't afraid to talk."

"You need someone with the gift of gab, you got the right girl," Sarah jokes.

"And for you, Sarah." Kate hands her the number ten. "Fly-half. Your job is important. Directing the backline and making big decisions."

Sarah is quiet for once. Her cheeks flush.

Tara is inside centre at number twelve and Lightning Lily is outside centre in number thirteen.

What a great pair of centres, I think.

"And number fifteen is for you, Maddy." Kate tosses me my jersey.

My heart races. Number fifteen means I'm starting. Starting fullback!

When everyone has a uniform, Hailey whistles to get our attention. "I'm meeting with the principal tomorrow. My aunt has volunteered to be our teacher sponsor. Aunt Jeanie is the last thing we need to be a full-fledged team!"

"And one other last thing." Kate holds up her hands for us to be quiet. "I've made some calls, and we're in."

"In what?" Everleigh asks.

"In the junior girls' rugby league. Registered! Our first game is next Thursday."

18 Curve BALL

The next morning before classes, Hailey, Everleigh, Sarah and I wait outside the principal's conference room. The big oak door is shut tight.

"Maybe he's in there," Everleigh whispers.

It's exactly seven forty-five, the arranged time.

Hailey knocks.

We can hear someone walking toward us.

That must be him, I think. But Ms. O comes around the corner. She stops abruptly when she sees us. We're wearing our jerseys. That was the plan — look like a team.

"Morning, girls," she smiles. "Lovely jerseys! May I ask why you're such early birds?"

Hailey tells her we have a meeting with Mr. Sharma, about her aunt being our teacher sponsor.

"Your aunt is a teacher?" Ms. O asks.

"Yep. Just moved here," says Hailey.

"So she's with the school district?"

"She just got here," Hailey replies. "Not yet."

A cloud falls over Ms. O's face. "Best of luck." She shuffles to her door and takes out a key. Her classroom is right there. Directly across the hall.

"You shouldn't have told her why we're meeting," Everleigh hisses. "She might barge in and rat us out."

Hailey eases the conference door open a crack and peeks in. "Nobody home." We file in.

There's a lingering trace of Mr. Sharma's yucky aftershave. And it's stuffy. I sit in one of the big armchairs and remember the last time we were here. These chairs try to swallow me. I tuck a foot under my butt.

"I can do the talking, if you want," says Hailey. She has letters from Kate and her aunt. There are three copies of each, outlining their qualifications and commitment. "You guys jump in if I miss something." Hailey sits across from me.

Sarah is serious. She opens her laptop. It has an outline of our budget and a bank balance.

There is a rumble of voices outside the door. It swings open and Mr. Sharma gives us a toothy smile. Mrs. Levens is right on his heels. "Good morning," they say in unison.

"Morning," we murmur.

Mrs. Levens struts to the end of the table clutching her ever-present bag of chopped vegetables. Mr. Sharma props the door open to let in some air. He sits at the head of the table and drops a massive binder on the glass tabletop.

I read the title. District Sport Policy.

He adjusts his tie so that it's perfectly centred. "You girls look great in your new jerseys. Very flashy," he says. "Let's get right to it." He looks at his watch, then points at Hailey's letters. "What do we have, Hailey?"

"We've been practicing at Rotary Park but not as a school team . . ." Hailey stalls.

"As a club," I say.

"I've heard about that," says Mr. Sharma. "But I see you're wearing our school crest and colours."

I hadn't thought of that.

"We're ready to be a school team. We've done everything." Hailey passes copies of the letters to Mr. Sharma and Mrs. Levens and explains what they are.

Both adults read. The wall clock ticks.

"Kate Kolisi looks good," says Mr. Sharma. "A certified coach, top notch first aid, very experienced. Your aunt?" Mr. Sharma asks, "Is she a district employee?"

"She's a teacher," Hailey says.

"With twelve years' experience," Everleigh adds.

"I'm afraid she needs to be employed by the district." Mr. Sharma looks at Hailey. "Does she have a position she's applying for?"

"I don't think so." Hailey shrugs one shoulder.

"Have you asked everyone on staff?"

"We've tried everyone," Everleigh pleads. "Couldn't we say Kate is coach and sponsor?"

"It's a district directive." Mr. Sharma taps the binder. "I'm sorry, I really am, but my hands are tied. Maybe Mrs. Levens and I could supervise an inter-squad game." He glances at her. "Mrs. Levens?"

My heart starts to sink. I really want to play rugby.

"I don't know," says Mrs. Levens. "A game of touch might be —"

Someone appears at the door. "May I interrupt?" It's Ms. O.

Oh no, I think. She's going to complain. We've been at Rotary Park, and we're wrecking the grass.

"I've got something . . ." She looks at the floor. "I need to tell you."

"Yes?" says Mr. Sharma. "Is this the right time?"

For a moment Ms. O seems stuck for words. She takes a long breath and stands as tall as she can. "I'd like to be teacher sponsor for girls' rugby."

19 The Old RUGBY JUICES

"What!" Everleigh blurts.

"Are you sure?" Mrs. Levens asks.

"This is a huge commitment," Mr. Sharma adds.

"I'm absolutely certain." Ms. O drops her cane against a chair as she sits, looking right at me. "When you first asked me, Maddy, I was reluctant. I said it's a big adventure for an old nag, but I've thought it through. And I've watched you girls." She places a hand on her chest. "I'm willing to be your teacher sponsor, if you'll have me."

Mr. Sharma asks, "Are you serious, Ms. Oblinski?"

"I've never been more serious." She has a smile on her face like I've never seen before. It's like she can't stop smiling.

"There's much to be considered." Mr. Sharma opens the binder to a sticky note. "First off, about field trips." He reads, "The teacher sponsor is fully responsible for each and every student from the time they leave the school until the student is returned to the care of their guardian."

"Of course," Ms. O beams. "Makes perfect sense."

"And the paperwork," Mr. Sharma continues reading. "All schedules, permission forms —"

Ms. O cuts him off. "Contact information and insurance forms must be up-to-date and kept in duplicate for the school principal and the athletic director." There's a mischievous glint in her eye.

Mr. Sharma looks surprised.

She leans toward him and whispers, "I've read the manual." She's having fun with this.

He says, "I worry about you in the weather. Rain or shine, with rugby, it's game on."

Ms. O doesn't hesitate. "I've got an umbrella large enough to shelter a family of four, a parka, the whole nine yards, so —"

"And your hip, Ms. Oblinski," says Mr. Sharma. "No offense, but can you keep up with these girls?"

"I wouldn't volunteer if I couldn't keep up, Ronald." She says his name like she's scolding him.

"We can try this," says Mr. Sharma, "on a trial basis." He nods at Ms. O.

She nods in agreement. "I've done a bit of research." She pulls a couple sheets of paper from a big manila envelope. "A branch of the provincial government provides funding for sports travel. This is the application."

Ms. O slides the papers across the table to Mrs. Levens. "It needs to be signed by the school's athletic director."

"I'm very familiar with it," says Mrs. Levens. But she gazes at the papers for a long moment. From down the hall I can hear the custodian's vacuum.

Finally Mrs. Levens says, "I suppose." She scribbles her name on the dotted line.

"So we've got your blessing?" Everleigh asks.

I can tell we're a long way from having her blessing. Mrs. Levens's lips have curled down like she just bit into a lemon.

"You've got my signature." She shoves the papers away. "Your ducks are in a row. All the boxes are ticked, so to speak." She stands and snatches her veggies off the table.

Mr. Sharma gets up and tucks the binder under his arm. "Best of luck, girls. You've done some good work." He heads for the door. "Let me know if I can help."

Mrs. Levens follows him.

"Well, that's that." Ms. O slaps her hands on the table.

"Thanks," says Hailey.

"Yeah, thanks." I don't know what else to say.

"But why were you spying on us?" asks Everleigh.

"Spying?" Ms. O looks confused.

"You were worried we'd wreck the grass," I offer. "Chew it up."

"Oh, yes," she says. "But, no, no. I didn't want you to get in trouble. With the City or the school."

"So why keep such a close eye on us?" asks Everleigh.

The Old Rugby Juices

"I couldn't get enough." She presses a palm to her chest. "Watching you play gives me a thrill. Gets the old rugby juices flowing."

"Rugby juices?" asks Everleigh.

I have to know. "Did you play rugby, Ms. O?"

Ms. O leans back in her chair and gazes out the window. "I did." She steeples her fingers. "I played in the first-ever women's game in BC. It was March 6, 1977. Douglas College against UBC." Her voice has a faraway quality like she's telling a long-forgotten story. "Douglas, my team, lost eight–nil. But it was a victory. A victory for both sides. Women's rugby came to life, that foggy grey afternoon."

Ms. O has a dreamy expression. For a moment it looks like she's off in another world, remembering.

"What position did you play?" Everleigh breaks the silence.

"I played hook." She sweeps a glance past all of us. "Smack dab in the middle of the scrum. I remember the newspaper headline the next day asked, 'Can You Believe Ladies' Rugby?' We were a lot like you girls. Some people thought girls shouldn't play rugby. No one thought we'd get a team going. But we did. And like you girls, we welcomed everyone. There was a girl that couldn't run a length of the field. By the end of the season, you know what?"

"What?" says Everleigh.

"She was one of our best players."

20 Game ON

It's game day and my stomach is in a knot. At three o'clock we flood onto the bus and cram into the back seats. The noise echoes off the steel walls. The bus driver blares the twang of country music on the radio. Everybody is yacking.

"There're eighteen of us," says Everleigh.

"Enough for three spares," I have to shout.

When Kate climbs the steps, Hailey stands and puts a finger to her lips. "*Shhhhh!*" The music stops and everyone shuts up.

"Congratulations, girls." Kate speaks from the front of the bus. "You guys have done the hard work. Today is the first Stampeders girls' game ever!"

The bus erupts into cheers and the thunder of foot stomps on the metal floor.

"The most important thing today," continues Kate. "I want you to make your tackles. A tackle is physical, sure," she says. "But the passion and desire comes from here." She points a finger to her head.

"And here." She points to her heart.

I know that I can tackle. My fists are clenched.

Ms. O is in the front seat. She clambers to her feet and turns to face us. "It's an hour to Central. Let's start thinking rugby."

Kate finds a seat halfway down the bus. She kneels on the seat, facing backward. "Okay, girls, quiz time," she calls out to us. "What's the difference between a ruck and a maul?"

"I know that one!" Everleigh shoots her hand up. "A ruck is when the tackled person is on the ground. She lets go of the ball because she has to, it's a rule. And over top of her, both teams fight for the ball."

Kate gives her a thumbs-up.

"A maul," Parm says, "is when the tackled player is still on her feet. Both sides are trying to get the ball and shove her down the field."

"That's great, Parm," says Kate. "How about this one? What happens if you carry the ball over your own goal line and touch the ball down?"

"Easy." I know this one. "No points are scored. It's a scrum for the other team on the five-metre line."

"I'm impressed," says Kate. "You guys are doing your homework. Who knows about the twenty-two-metre line?"

"Got it." Hailey runs a hand over the shaved side of her head. "If you kick the ball out from behind the twenty-two, the line-out is upfield. Where the ball goes out. But if you kick it out from in front of the twenty-two, the line-out is from where you kicked."

"Wow," says Kate. "You guys rock."

An hour later, we pull into the Central Secondary parking lot. I get my first glimpse of the opposition. They've got flashy blue warm-up jackets. They're on the field doing a fast-paced drill, balls flying in every direction.

"They look pretty good," says Tara.

A tremor of excitement races up my spine. My stomach does a little flip.

"Fire up, girls!" Hailey calls out.

"Let's go get 'em!" says Ms. O. She gives us each a high-five as we walk past.

I'm last off the bus. I can't stop watching the Central girls. They're making snappy passes and looking very professional. I realize I'm holding my breath.

★★★

Just before the game, Kate pulls us all into a huddle. We lock our arms tight around each other's waists and shoulders. It's a warm spring day and I'm shoulder to shoulder with my besties. But my stomach is flipping. I've never been this nervous.

Hailey jogs to centre and shakes hands with the referee. Then she shakes with the Central captain. I watch the ref flip a coin.

Hailey trots back. We're still locked in our huddle.

"We won the toss. We kick off," says Hailey. "The ref knows it's our first game, but you know the rule. Only I talk to the ref."

We line up to kick off. I size up their fullback across the field. She's my number one responsibility today. She stands with her hands on her hips, wide stance. She looks super confident.

I watch her tighten her long blonde ponytail. She turns my way and digs her eyes into me. She pops out her mouth guard, glares and spits.

Kate's words echo in my mind. *Make your tackles.*

Hailey kicks off a nice high ball. One of their big forwards catches and charges straight upfield. Bobby wraps her up, but the girl keeps pumping her legs. Her teammates latch on and drive her upfield. One of them rips the ball away and barges into Sarah.

I stay deep, to cover if they kick. That's my job. But all I can do is watch and I'm dying to get some action.

Central keeps the ball tight with their forwards. They're taking short bursting runs and grinding their way down the field. Finally one of them passes slightly forward. The ref blows the whistle.

"Set scrum." He holds a palm up in our direction. "Your put-in, red."

Everleigh feeds the ball into the scrum. Central heaves forward, but we hold our ground. Everleigh picks up from Hailey's feet at the back of the scrum and fires a long pass to Sarah. She is deep in the pocket, well behind the scrum. She has time to thump a good boot downfield.

Their fullback catches and takes off at a sprint. She beats our first line of defence. She's in open field, coming right at me.

21 ALL HEART

My heart skips. Adrenaline races through me.

This is it!

The fullback races toward me. Her eyes are fixed wide. She's not going to pass.

I drop into a strong crouch. All my muscles are coiled tight as a spring. She's going to try to run over me. I shoot myself at her, shoulder first. Her knee cracks my cheek but I get my arms around her legs. She plows forward.

I start slipping off her. Losing my grip. One of her boots thumps me solid in the chest. I clamp onto her foot. It's my last chance. I squeeze my eyes closed and clench my teeth. I've got a vice grip, jamming her boot to the middle of my chest.

Finally she goes down. I pop up to get my hands on the ball. The next blue player is a solid flanker. She drives me back.

"Well done!" Ms. O calls from the sidelines. "Brilliant tackle, Madison!"

The Central scrum-half picks up and boots the ball deep. It rolls all the way into our in-goal. One of their wingers outraces everyone and dives on it.

The whistle blasts. "That's a try!"

We kick off and Sarah leaps high to make the catch. She dashes thirty metres into their end and throws Tara a long pass. Tara breaks one tackle, then another. She gets hit hard, but pops up an offload to Ava. Ava gets driven out of bounds just metres from the goal line.

Central wins the line-out. Their fly-half puts up a huge punt that goes way over my head. I sprint after the ball. But the Central outside centre is ultra-fast. She chases down the ball and hacks it forward with a little kick. The ball hops up for their winger. Right into her hands! She dashes forty metres untouched and they score a second try. It's fourteen–nil at the break.

"You guys are all heart." Kate pulls us in tight.

I'm feeling good about my first half. I caught a high ball under pressure. I've had ball carriers run at me three times and haven't missed a tackle!

"You girls are playing stuck-in, gutsy rugby." Kate thumps a fist to her chest. "I couldn't be prouder."

Well into the second half there's a line-out, Central's throw in. Ava makes a steal and Everleigh throws a long pass to Sarah at fly-half. I come in right next to Sarah and catch her perfect pass. The blue shirts are shooting up fast on defence. I see the gap between the centres. I slow a step and boot a grubber through.

All Heart

Their fullback cuts hard toward the ball. But Tara, Lily and I are all racing for it full speed. It seems like the kick has too much on it, maybe too long. At the perfect split-second Lily stretches out and scoops it up off the ground.

Their defence doesn't have a chance. Lily races ten metres. She dives over the line and scores our first try. Our girls mob her. It's a full team hug. I'm smothered between Sarah and Bobbi.

"What a play!" shouts Hailey. Her armpit is jammed in my face, but I've never felt better.

The final score is nineteen to five. We clap each other off the field. Their coach wheels a giant cooler of drinks to the sideline.

"You guys are hard runners." The Central fullback touches her plastic bottle to mine. "And tough tacklers."

Their captain gets everyone's attention. "Thanks for coming all the way out to play the game. It was tough out there. We had to really dig in and work our butts off." She gives Hailey a Central T-shirt. Hailey presents her with one of ours.

Afterward, in the change room, Kate tells us, "I'm super proud of the way you guys played today. You've got something I can't teach. Either you have it or you don't. Courage. You guys are all heart."

"Think of everything you learned today," says Ms. O. "A rugby team is a building process. And you ladies have a solid foundation."

"And you've got a solid bank account," says Kate. "Thanks to a very special someone."

"Who was it?" asks Everleigh. "Who made the big anonymous donation?"

Kate drops a hand on Ms. O's shoulder.

"Was it you, Ms. O?" Sarah asks.

Ms. O's cheeks flush to pink. "What else do I have to spend my money on?"

On the way to the bus, a man with a walrus moustache holds up his hand for me to stop, like a traffic guard.

"Could I get a quote?" he asks. "I'm with the paper."

"Sure."

"No offense, but I couldn't help noticing your size." He twists the end of his moustache between thumb and forefinger. "What's your biggest challenge out there?"

"No big challenge," I say. "Bit of an advantage really."

"How's that?"

"Coach says get low to make your tackles. I'm already there." I smile. He points his camera and it *click, clicks*.

On the bus Kate hands a clipboard around. "I'm setting up a webpage for our team. I want names, positions, height, weight. And some fun stuff. What's your pregame meal? Rugby superstition? Your nickname?"

"Pregame meal?" says Sarah. "Plate full of scrap iron, maybe a few nails."

When I get the clipboard I pencil in my weight. I haven't told anyone, but I've gained a full five pounds. And I'm an inch taller!

ACKNOWLEDGEMENTS

I'd like to thank Kayla Moleschi for allowing me to feature her in Maddy's story and for giving me free rein to interpret her famous try in Dubai against New Zealand. In this story, Kayla is a source of motivation and excitement for Maddy and the girls. In reality, she is a source of motivation and excitement for hundreds of us.

A special thanks to my son Cole Levitt, who is an ongoing sounding board for me, providing feedback on technical aspects of play-by-play action and always giving me an accurate lens into the modern game.

It was a pleasure working with the people at Lorimer. A big shout out to Kat Mototsune, who once again guided me patiently and professionally through the steps of editing. Thank you, Carrie Gleason, for your knowledge and guidance, and in the long run, for making Maddy's story far more intriguing.

Thanks to Carly Walters for helping me understand what it is like to be a woman of smaller stature, playing rugby powerfully and successfully at a very high level. Maddy's newspaper quote is all Carly!

Nina Johnson's passion for writing is contagious. With two simple words, "what if," she opened all the imaginative doors I could have asked for. Thank you, George Johnson, for recognizing my work with the English Modern Language Award and, in turn, giving me a much appreciated leg up.

Acknowledgements

Much appreciation to Lorraine for being my devoted beta reader and for always believing in me. Without our endless "readings," *Rugby Rookies* would never have made it past the first draft.